"Stop doing that."

"Doing what?" He offered a smug grin. "Cleaning up after you?"

"No. Making me lose control."

"Is that what I do to you?" Damn, but he hoped so.

Her breathing deepened, her chest expanding with her heavy breaths. "Yes."

Things were progressing right on track. "Good. I think you need to lose control, Red."

"No, I don't. That's not a good thing." She pushed against his chest but the gesture seemed halfhearted.

"I think it's a very good thing."

"Ha. You would. You're a man." Her eyes glittered like whiskey in a cut-glass tumbler. "I think *you* need to lose control."

To prove her point, she wrapped her hands around the back of his neck and tugged his face down to hers.

* * *

Redeemed by the Cowgirl is part of the Red Dirt Royalty series—

T

Dear Reader,

Writers often get asked where we get our ideas and how we pick the characters we write about. I joke about my coffee-swilling Muse (named Iffy), who runs with scissors, because I don't always have an answer that would make sense to a nonwriter. In the case of Roxanne Rowland, she strutted into my imagination one day and demanded a book. I wrote down a few notes and promptly delegated her to the back burner. For several years. Because I had no idea what her story might be.

Did I mention Roxie was patient? She was—up to a point. When it came time to find a heroine for Cash Barron, the baddest of the billionaire brothers, Roxie held up her hand—not to be recognized but to deliver a classic "Gibbs slap" to the back of my head. I'm slow. It took me a while to figure out what she wanted, but she's right. She was meant to be Cash's happily-ever-after.

Watching her stretch her wings while he confronted his demons turned this book into a labor of love full of surprises and a couple of detours I didn't see coming. I hope you have half as much fun reading their story as I did writing it.

Love can conquer all!

Silver James

SILVER JAMES

REDEEMED BY THE COWGIRL

HARLEQUIN® DESIRE

Recycling programs
for this product may
not exist in your area.

ISBN-13: 978-0-373-83834-9

Redeemed by the Cowgirl

Printed in U.S.A.

www.Harlequin.com

Silver James likes walks on the wild side and coffee. Okay. She LOVES coffee. A cowgirl at heart, she's been an army officer's wife and mom, and worked in the legal field, fire service and law enforcement. Now retired from the real world, she lives in Oklahoma, spending her days writing with the assistance of two Newfoundlands, the cat who rules them all and the characters living in her imagination.

Books by Silver James

Harlequin Desire

Red Dirt Royalty

Cowgirls Don't Cry
The Cowgirl's Little Secret
The Boss and His Cowgirl
Convenient Cowgirl Bride
Redeemed by the Cowgirl

Visit her Author Profile page at Harlequin.com, or silverjames.com, for more titles.

To Clary. You know why.
And to my dream editor, Charles.
You know why, too.
Also to Stacy and Tahra, and the
whole fantastic Harlequin Desire team!
Y'all are made of awesomesauce.

One

Cash Barron was a man who understood duty—especially to his family. Unlike his brothers. Staring out the window of his twin's apartment on the fiftieth floor of Barron Crown Hotel and Casino in Las Vegas, he did his best to stuff his anger into a corner of his mind. He'd watched his three older brothers turn their backs and walk away from the very thing that made them Barrons—their loyalty to one another. Even his twin, Chase, had chosen a woman so completely unsuitable that Cash could barely comprehend their marriage. And now Chase and Savannah were about to celebrate the first anniversary of their quickie Vegas wedding.

A sharp rap on the door jerked his attention from the vista outside the window. Bridger Tate, his cousin and second-in-command, entered without invitation. He didn't like the look on the man's face.

"What?"

"Last night's video from the casino floor has been analyzed."

A series of curse words ricocheted through his brain but he refrained from speaking them. "Is it them?"

Bridge looked angry but resigned. "Yeah. Tucker isolated images of the Rowland clan on the casino floor."

Tucker Tate was Bridger's brother and vice president of Barron Entertainment, the media and hotel conglomerate that was Chase's domain. They'd been dealing with a security problem at the casino for almost a year. As president of Barron Security Services, all problems—from the security detail for his brother Senator Clay Barron to the theft of oilfield pipe from a Barron Energy drilling site—landed on his desk. The occasional missing cow from the ranch, the odd employee embezzlement, the more frequent crackpot sending threatening emails—these bucks all stopped with him. It was his job to protect his family, even from themselves.

"Cash?"

Glancing up, he realized he'd tuned out Bridger's play-by-play. "Sorry. What were you saying?"

"Tuck did a good job isolating the Rowlands."

"Are they all present and accounted for?"

"Yup. Max, Alex and Ajax, Braxton, Dexter. The king of cons and his larcenous princes. I had IT highlight their positions in each of the videos."

Cash huffed out a breath that was a thinly disguised

sigh. He strode to Chase's in-home office, settled heavily at the desk and called up the info on the giant monitor. He leaned back, eyes tracking the glowing orbs highlighting faces on the screen.

Bridger settled a hip on the corner of the desk and twisted his head to see the monitor. "I have our IT team checking footage from Scottsdale, Nashville, Miami and New Orleans."

"What's their objective?"

"Who knows? Seems they really like Barron properties, though."

"Jolly."

"Yeah, figured that would please you."

"Are we the marks or is it a guest?"

"Probably both."

Cash closed his eyes and rubbed the back of his neck. Could it get any more complicated?

Roxanne Rowland lined her lips with red pencil before adding bright red gloss. The woman in the mirror staring back at her was a stranger. Dragging fingers through her red hair, she fluffed the waves, startled anew by the bright color tipping her nails. She wasn't used to the manicure, either. Dark, smoky shadows fringed her eyes, making them sparkle like amber. She refused to wear the tinted contacts sitting in a case on the counter.

Smoothing down the borrowed body-hugging black dress, she opened the bathroom door and collided with her older brother. His fingers gripped her biceps none too gently. "Time to go, Rox." He studied her a moment. "You didn't wear the contacts."

She winced at the accusatory tone in his voice. "They hurt and make my eyes water. I had to redo my makeup three times before I gave up."

He squeezed her arm as he strode away, pulling her along. She wobbled on the stiletto heels and teetered for a moment as she scrambled to find her balance. The high heels were as foreign to her as the rest of her getup. She wore jeans and boots. Not haute couture. Especially not a dress that cost close to a month's salary—a dress she'd been told to tuck the tag inside and not to get dirty. That meant it would be returned to the store for a credit.

"What's going on, Dex?"

"You don't need to know, little sister."

"Yes, I do."

"Max is working."

Maximilian Rowland—her father and sire of her four older brothers, Lex, Jax, Brax and Dex—whom they never called "Dad."

"That doesn't explain why *I'm* here. I don't work with him."

"You do now." His voice remained implacable as he ushered her out of the hotel room. "This is big, Rox, and you'll do your duty to the family. Or else."

Or else? What did that mean? Dex didn't enlighten her as they rode down in the elevator. When he'd picked her up at Las Vegas's McCarran International Airport, all he'd said was that their father needed her help, and it was time to take her place in the family.

"Stop fidgeting."

"I can't help it."

Dex cut his eyes in her direction and smirked. "What's wrong, your feet hurt?"

"As a matter of fact." Her feet didn't just hurt, they ached like someone was shoving cold needles into her toes and hammering her arches with rusty nails. "You try wearing these shoes for five minutes."

"I'm a guy. I don't wear heels."

"So?"

"So, you're a girl. You do."

"No, I don't. I—" She didn't get to finish her argument. The elevator doors opened and Dex grabbed her arm, jerking her out into a swirl of color and noise. He guided her into a corner, his gaze fixed on the ceiling.

"Stand here until one of us comes to get you."

"What? No—"

"Shut up, Roxie. Do as you're told."

"You are not the boss of me, Dexter."

"Tonight I am. Shut up and listen. There's a man at the blackjack table. He has a propensity for redheads. Tall, curvy redheads." He flicked the strap of her dress so it sagged off the curve of her shoulder. "When the time comes, you will sashay that sweet ass of yours to Max. You will ignore Max but you will make nice to the man next to him. Understood?

"No."

"Tough. Just do as you're told. You flirt. You distract. And you get him to take you up to his room. You get him naked and we'll do the rest."

"Now you wait just a minute, Dexter Row—"

He pushed her back into the corner, eyes hard. "You've had it easy all your life, baby girl. Time to pay up. We told Max he screwed up sending you off to those snooty schools instead of teaching you what you needed to know about the business. That ends tonight. Starting now, you'll do your duty to this family."

Dex draped a heavy necklace around her throat. Colored diamonds and old gold. He bent to her ear. "There's more where this came from—all hidden where you won't find the evidence, but the cops will. You try to walk away or turn us in? They'll know just how deeply involved you are."

"That's blackmail." Her voice remained remarkably steady despite the fear zinging through her.

"Welcome to the family, little sister."

With those parting words, he disappeared into the crowd bustling around the entrance to the casino floor. When they'd arrived at the Crown Hotel and Casino that afternoon, she'd been excited. The resort was one of the jewels on the Las Vegas Strip. Like the naive twit she evidently was, she thought she was coming for a vacation at the luxurious hotel. Yeah, no.

She slipped her feet out of the heels and almost whimpered in relief when the thick rug cushioned her toes. She wasn't sure she believed Dex's threat. He'd always been something of a bully—a fact she'd put down to him being the youngest brother. Sibling rivalry rolled downhill. Alexander—Lex, her oldest brother—had always been aloof. He'd been thirteen when she was born, and they had nothing in common. By the time she'd turned five, he was already traveling with Max. Ajax, two years younger than Lex, was the next oldest. Tall, handsome and gregarious, Jax was a charmer. He'd always attracted the opposite sex. He and Braxton were what were sometimes referred to as Catholic twins—barely nine months apart. Brax was the scholar, always reading and studying. Wickedly intelligent, he had an innate ability to plan. Then there was Dex. He'd been five when Roxie came along, and he'd pretty much hated her from the beginning.

Roxie jerked her thoughts away from her family and concentrated on how she could get out of this mess. She didn't doubt for a minute that Dex would carry through with his threat and not only set her up but make sure she took the fall. She knew that from experience. At the moment, she had no choice but to follow orders until she could figure out their endgame and how to avoid involvement.

"Get your shoes on, girl."

Startled, she retreated deeper into the corner and squinted at Lex. At 35, he was debonair and aloof, and he scared her just a little. Okay, if she was honest, a lot. He might have been absent—like Max—for most of her childhood, but when he was around, he was as much a father figure as Max had been.

"I don't want to do this, Lex. Whatever *this* is." She made air quotes for emphasis.

"Don't care what you want, Roxanne. You're doing it. Get your shoes on and get out there. You make that smart mouth of yours pouty, bat your lashes and get the mark up to his room."

"Or else? Dex already threatened me with that. I'm not impressed."

He slid his big hand around her throat, and she gulped but raised her chin. "Not telling you again. Get to work." Squeezing his fingers for good measure, he didn't let her go until she had both shoes on her feet and was wobbling into the throng of vacationers.

She was terrified of falling flat on her face, arms and legs akimbo, her tush displayed in the air and her thong hiding nothing from the crowd of onlookers. "Slow down," she hissed over her shoulder at Lex. He didn't, the hand at the small of her back pushing her harder. "If I fall off these darn shoes and break my ankle, the great con will be a bust."

Cash rubbed his eyes, a dull headache caused by staring at the bank of security monitors throbbing at the base of his skull. Tucker handed him a cup of coffee and a bottle of painkillers. He tossed back a couple of the pills and chased them with the hot black liquid.

"When did you tumble onto their presence?" Cash didn't take his eyes from the live footage.

"Yesterday when they checked in. That new facial recognition software you had installed works like a charm. I have footage if you want to see." Tucker watched the monitors, too.

"Just give me the rundown."

"Max arrived first. Had reservations for a mini-suite under the name Grant Franklin."

Cash scrubbed at his forehead with the heel of one hand. "And his sons?"

"Alexander and Ajax checked in together. Another mini-suite. Hamilton and Jackson Grant."

"Please tell me you're joking."

"Nope." Tuck's voice hardened.

"Great. Go on."

"Braxton checked in about an hour later. Lincoln Washington. And then Dexter checked in this afternoon. Reservations were for Mr. and Mrs. Franklin Cleveland."

Cash sat up straight, whipping around to stare at the other man. "Hamilton, Jackson, Grant, Lincoln, Washington, Franklin and Cleveland. Now they're just rubbing our noses in it." His cousin looked confused so he laid it out. "Those are presidential last names. All of them. Except Franklin. But ol' Ben's still on the hundred-dollar bill."

"It's all about the money."

"Yeah. Wait. Dexter brought a woman?" Cash pushed out of the chair. "Do you have a picture of her?"

"No. He checked in alone, was up in his room for about forty-five minutes and then left in a cab he caught at the front entrance. He hasn't been back since."

"You sure of that?" Cash walked to a monitor and tapped it. "That's Dexter at the roulette table."

"How the hell—"

Bridger walked up to them and cut his brother off. "We have a gap in the security surveillance somewhere. We'll find it, Tuck. Sorry I'm late for the party, Cash. I was double-checking footage."

"I want eyes on all of the Rowlands. Max is at the high-stakes blackjack table. Alex walked out about five minutes ago, after Dexter tossed him a high sign. Ajax and Braxton are roaming around on the slot machine floor." Cash returned to his chair and swiveled it around. "I want our guys on them, Bridger." He held up a hand to stop Tucker's rebuttal. "Your security is good. Heck, we hired and trained them, but they look like casino security. My guys won't."

Bridger offered a feral grin to Tucker. "Little brother, you pick my guys out, I'll buy you the biggest steak they have at the Barron House."

The radio at Cash's elbow hissed. "I have target two in sight. He's with a woman. Redhead. Black dress. Lobby entrance."

Cash's eyes swept the bank of monitors until he picked out Alex Rowland. His eyes locked on the woman preceding the thief. She was tall but not slender. No, she definitely had curves in all the places a woman should, but she still looked sleek in the short cocktail dress. Her auburn hair was a mass of wavy curls, but he couldn't tell the color of her eyes through the grainy camera lens. He stared at her, a memory swimming in the back of his mind. He knew her from somewhere.

Alex peeled away and Braxton took his place, herding the woman toward the table where Max sat, relaxed and cheerful. She stumbled and Cash found himself reaching forward as if to catch her. Braxton made no move to assist, and it was a stranger who offered a steadying hand. He managed to read her lips, the words and expression easy to translate. "Pardon me. I'm so sorry," she mouthed before Braxton swept her along in front of him.

"Bridge, pull in some markers. Find out when the Rowlands added a woman to their crew. I want to know who she is."

"On it."

Cash continued to study the woman. She looked… uncomfortable. Unsure. If it was an act, it was a good one. She ended up squeezed between Max and the man next to him at the table, all but sprawled in the man's lap. Something hot and angry lanced through him. Keying the camera on her face, he could see that she looked young and scared despite the getup. That didn't fit the Rowlands' MO at all. That odd sense of recognition continued to niggle at him and he sorted through memories of all the women he knew. He'd figure it out sooner or later.

He'd been so intent on the woman—girl—he'd lost track of the other Rowlands. "Where's Alex? And where did Ajax and Dexter disappear to?"

Various scenes flickered on the monitors mounted to the wall in front of him and a lot of cuss words filtered into muttered conversations as Chase's security staff combed the screens for a sighting. Something popped, and then there was a hum like a generator winding down. Moments later, lights dimmed, monitors died and the room was plunged into darkness.

Cash was out of his chair and headed toward the door as backup lighting kicked in. He tapped the emergency code into the keypad and had to shove the door open when the lock clicked. He heard Bridger shouting behind him.

"Lock down the counting room and the vault. Deploy personnel to all the exits."

Knowing Bridge would take control of the security room, Cash sprang into action. He needed to get his hands on one of the Rowlands. And he definitely wanted to get his hands on the red-haired woman.

The lights went out and the packed casino floor erupted into pandemonium. Women squealed. Men shouted. Other voices rose, yelling above the melee in an effort to restore order. Lights from cell phones added ghostly illumination to the scene as emergency lighting flickered on.

Someone gripped Roxie's arm and jerked. She attempted to pull away but hearing her name growled shocked her into compliancy. Max. She tripped after him, trying to stay upright. Blasted shoes. She hobbled in her father's wake, then he shoved her at Dex with a muffled, "Get her undercover."

The next thing she knew, she was tossed over her brother's shoulder like a sack of flour, and no amount of beating against his back made him release her. She tried to kick her legs but his arm was an iron band across her knees. When they reached one of the exit doors, he set her down and backed her against the wall. A moment later, the door slammed open, missing her by a hair.

She watched a tall man sprint through the exit. Dark hair, broad shoulders, a shadowed jawline. His suit was likely hand-tailored. Roxie wondered who he was as Dex disappeared into the stairwell and the door closed.

She pulled on the handle, panicked now that she was alone. The door didn't budge. She had to get away.

Roxie turned, feeling the blood drain from her face. She recognized the man now. Cash Barron, standing there, bigger'n Dallas. She whirled to run the other direction only to be brought up short by two security guards who could play middle linebacker for the Dallas Cowboys. She pivoted very slowly to face the man she'd never been able to get out of her fantasies. She was in so much trouble now.

"Well, well, well. What do we have here?"

Two

As soon as Cash saw her up close, he remembered who she was—or who he thought she'd been. Anne Landerson—a slightly clueless student who'd been involved with the theft of some jewels and fine art from his great-aunt Elizabeth. He reached out to snag her but she charged, ducking under his arm and diving into the crowd milling around the lobby. He plowed after her but she was gone, running right out of her shoes. He was left with a pair of killer stilettos in a color his sisters-in-law described as "Do-Me Red." Like a whiff of smoke, she was gone.

Two hours later, he was no closer to capturing any of them. Despite the lockdown, the Rowlands had escaped, as had the girl. Frustrated at every turn, Cash threw in the allegorical towel and returned to Oklahoma City.

Cash spent the week chasing shadows, but no concrete leads had popped up. Neither had the Rowlands. Frustrated, he sat in his office staring at the designer high heels displayed on his desk. How the hell did a woman walk on stilts like them? Then he remembered the stumbling gait of the woman in the security footage. A woman dressed to the nines, with makeup meant for seduction, wearing a black cocktail dress that hugged her curves like a lover. A curious dichotomy. He'd pulled the file on his aunt's case, one of the first Barron Security had handled after he took over.

The girl had claimed to know nothing about the stolen goods—only that she'd received a package in the mail and the items had been inside. She'd been scared, panic and apologies reflected in her huge amber eyes—eyes Cash hadn't forgotten in the six years since the incident. The school's headmistress and the lawyer who'd showed up had met with the prosecutor and a deal had been worked out. Seemed the kid was probably an innocent dupe so Barron Security signed off on community service and recovery of the property.

Now he had another problem. He'd run a search on Anne Landerson. She didn't exist. There was no record of her in any databases his team could access. Bridger was calling in favors to check those they couldn't without special dispensation. In the meantime, he had to focus on the Rowlands. He was no closer to discovering why they were targeting Barron properties and what their endgame could be.

Twice now, this girl had been in the Rowlands' crosshairs. Why? Was she with one of the brothers? That created a tangled knot of thoughts. For reasons he couldn't identify, Chase didn't like the idea of her belonging to someone.

A brusque tap on his door had him looking up as Bridger entered.

"Please tell me you've found something."

His second-in-command shook his head, a hangdog expression on his face. "Nothing with FBI or Treasury. We even checked Interpol. The Rowlands are everywhere, but the girl? She's a ghost, at least under that name."

Cash leaned back in the massive leather desk chair and scratched at his cheek. His dark stubble was becoming a beard, a decision he made after he'd impersonated his twin in an attempt to make Chase and his wife separate, and realized how simple it was. "Maybe we're looking at this wrong."

"How so?"

"Could she have been the mark?"

Before Bridger could answer, his phone pinged. He checked the screen and a huge smile creased his cheeks. "Bingo. We found her."

Bridger pressed some buttons on his phone and a second later, a link popped up on Cash's computer monitor. He clicked on it and waited as the tab opened. There she was. Sort of. His brow furrowed as he stared at a face familiar yet that of a stranger. He read off the information.

"Roxanne Rosetta Rowland. Bachelor's degree in history, followed by a master's in museum studies."

Cash continued skimming the information. "She graduated from the University of Central Oklahoma?"

"Yup. And with that information, we should be able to find out where she's currently living and working, and why there's no record tying her to the Rowlands, especially since she's using their name."

"I want to know everything there is to know about her." Cash rubbed his chin. Oh, yeah. He wanted every last detail about Roxanne Rowland, especially where she'd been and what she'd done since that interview at the Fairfax Police Department. Man, but he'd been a fool to believe her sob story and not follow up, despite assertions from the school that she was a victim. Innocents didn't use fake names. Now he'd have the facts before the day was out.

Roxie paced the confines of her cluttered office. No one in her family had contacted her. She'd managed to get to her room in Vegas, grab her stuff—sans the blackmail items—and run. Ha! She knew all their tricks, and had found the incriminating evidence and deposited it in the lost and found box on a maid's cart on her way out. She'd caught the first flight out of Las Vegas, then made her way home.

Every time her phone dinged with a text message, she jumped. Was it one of her brothers? But there had been no phone calls. No emails. Nothing. Aggravated, she'd put her research skills to work. What she'd discovered about her family left her worried, feeling stupid and more than a little angry. She'd guessed they walked the wrong side of the line. Con men. Grifters. But like an ostrich with her head buried, she'd had no clue how illicit their activities were. Her father and brothers were wanted by the FBI and Interpol for fraud, theft and questioning in a murder.

"What have y'all dragged me into?" she muttered as she paced. And what did the Barrons have to do with it? Nobody took on the Barron family and won. Everyone at Reade-Cannon-Mansfield was in awe of the family people called Red Dirt Royalty. She wouldn't be surprised if the advertising firm had originally coined the phrase. While she really wanted to work in a museum, she loved her job as corporate archivist for the ad agency. She didn't want to jeopardize her position by tangling with the Barrons.

So what could she do? Going to the police was a bad idea. One, she had no clue what her family had done— if anything—and two, she'd likely be considered an accessory. If the police got involved, she could kiss any chance of a career goodbye.

She clutched her cell phone in her hand and stared at it. Should she call Max and ask him what was going on? Would he tell her? She bit her bottom lip in indecision. Scrolling to his name on her contact list, her thumb hovered over the call button. When the phone vibrated in her hand, she almost dropped it. Fumbling and juggling, she got it back in her grip and stared at the text message from Brax.

FORGET U EVER WENT TO VEGAS

She texted back frantically. What's going on?

NOT A WORD TO ANY1 ROX BAD THINGS HAPPEN
IF U TALK

I want to know what's happening!

WILL CALL WHEN WE NEED U JUST REMEMBER
FAMILY IS EVERYTHING

Family is everything? That was rich. Growing up,
she spent every Christmas alone at boarding school.
The one time they'd remembered her birthday, it had
been to hide their ill-gotten gains. And graduations?
Ha! Their idea of family and hers were oceans apart.

She stared at the screen. Wait. Bad things would happen if she talked? What did that mean? She panicked for
a moment, sinking onto her chair and putting her head
between her knees. When she stopped seeing stars, she
straightened. Her father and brothers were criminals.
And they were up to their necks in something involving
the Barrons—something they wanted her in the middle
of. That was so not going to happen.

"What to do, what to do?" she mumbled, standing
to pace again. One of the open tabs on her computer
browser caught her gaze. A web search for "Barron
Companies."

Dropping into her chair, she scooted it up to the desk
and began investigating. Five minutes later, she had a
phone number for Barron Security Services, at the helm
of which was CEO Cash Barron. She hadn't known who
he was back when she was sixteen and he'd stood in that
dingy interview room at the Fairfax Police Department.

But she'd never forgotten him. He'd starred in some of her more…lurid fantasies over the years. Should she call him? What would she say?

She needed a plan.

Cash put his best tracer on Roxanne Rowland. The information they'd discovered did not mesh with what he knew about the rest of the family. The girl lived in a cheap apartment in the northwest part of town and worked at Reade-Cannon-Mansfield, the premier advertising firm based in Oklahoma City. He'd made some phone calls to the Barron account executive at RCM to get a rundown on her. According to his investigation of the Rowlands, Max and the boys lived the high life. From the French Riviera, to the luxury hotels of Dubai and Hong Kong, to the Gold Coast of Florida, the Hamptons, Aspen. Every playground of the rich and famous had been a hunting ground for the larcenous clan. None of that jibed with the information they'd dug up on Roxanne.

His door burst open and Bridger stood there with a shit-eating grin. "You aren't going to believe who's on line one." His cousin nodded toward the phone console on the desk.

Cash arched a brow, waiting for Bridger to fill him in. He didn't have to wait long.

"A woman wanting to speak to whoever is in charge of casino security. The call was routed to Cheri. When she asked the caller's name, the twit gave it to her. Roxanne Rowland."

Suspicious by nature, Cash reined in the surge of

adrenaline spiking through him at the news. "What are the odds, Bridge?"

"High enough I wouldn't lay a bet on 'em. That said, we don't have anything to lose. I've already started the trace on the call. I can keep her on the line long enough to pinpoint her location."

Cash motioned him closer, and before hitting the line to put it on speakerphone, said, "You take the call."

"Bridger Tate. How can I help you?"

"Um…" Several muffled breaths puffed through the speaker. "Uh…hi. I…are you the one in charge of security for the Crown Casino out in Las Vegas?"

"Yes."

"Uh…you said your name is Tate?" The voice on the other end sounded hesitant.

"That's right. Bridger Tate. I'm vice president of BSS."

"Oh. Okay. That's okay then. I guess."

"Is there a reason you're calling, ma'am?"

"Oh. Roxie. Er, Roxanne. Roxanne Rowland. You don't know me or anything."

Cash made a circling motion with his hand, indicating Bridger should move things along.

"Should I know you, Ms. Rowland?"

"No." The word came out forcefully. "I mean, no." Softer this time. "I don't think so. I…look, I'm sorry. This was a bad idea."

"Don't hang up!" Cash's order cut through the air. "This is Cash Barron."

"Oh." The single syllable all but trembled as it sighed through the speaker.

"Why are you calling, Ms. Rowland?"

"My family…you see, they…"

They what? he wanted to shout. Her father and brothers were criminal scum and she had to be calling on their behalf. What sort of scam were they trying to set up? "I don't have all day, Ms. Rowland. There must be a reason you're calling. Get to it."

"Oh, okay. Yes. Well, see… I'd like to meet with you. Explain in person." Her voice grew a little stronger. The woman was a helluva actress.

"Explain what?"

"Can we meet somewhere?"

"I'll be happy to set up an appointment here in our offices." And he'd have the cops on speed dial to take her into custody.

"I… I'm not sure that would be a good idea." She inhaled deeply and blew out the breath. "Oh, never mind. This was a stupid idea. I'm sorry to have bothered you."

"Ms. Rowland," Cash snarled. "Roxanne."

"I don't know what's going on. I don't know what they're doing. Only that it's bad. I'm sure of it. It was stupid to call you. I just… When I saw you in Vegas, and recognized you… I thought maybe…oh, heck. I don't know what I thought."

"Come to my office, Roxanne. We'll talk."

"No. I don't know if they're following me."

"Who?"

"My…never mind. I…look, I'll be at the…at the—" She cleared her throat. "Cyrano's. At Thunder River Casino. You know where it is, right? Eight o'clock tonight." Muffled voices sounded in the background. "I have to go. I'll be there. For an hour."

SILVER JAMES   29

The dead line hummed over the speaker. Cash hit the button to end the call. Oh, yeah. He knew where the nightclub was all right. He stared at his cousin. "What's your take on this?"

Bridger lifted his shoulders and dropped them, his expression perplexed. "Your guess is as good as mine. I do find it interesting that we hit pay dirt with our search on her and she just happens to call. Out of the blue."

"Don't trust coincidences?"

"Nope."

"Neither do I."

"Then again, Cash, maybe we shouldn't look a gift horse in the mouth."

"Maybe. Maybe not."

"You'll meet her?"

Cash curled his lips into a sarcastic smile that didn't reach his eyes but coated his voice. "What do you think? I mean, gift horse and all that."

"Yeah, I figured. I'll arrange backup."

Backup was easy. Barron Security was the authority in casino operations, and in addition to the Barron family properties, they had contracts with most of the tribal entities in Oklahoma. Meaning they'd have their own security force in place at Thunder River.

After Bridger walked out, Cash studied Roxanne's driver's license. Fresh-faced, her red hair a tangle of wisps and waves, eyes the color of the aged whiskey he liked to drink. With a click of the mouse, he displayed the clearest photo he had of her from the Barron Casino. Smoky eye shadow smudging her lids. Kiss-me red lips. Heightened color on her cheeks. The girl in the first photo appeared sure of herself, almost cocky, but with a sweetness under the surface. The second? She looked like a kid playing dress-up. Who was the real Roxanne Rowland? Cash planned to find out. And would in a matter of hours.

He couldn't wait.

Three

Cash studied the monitors in the Thunder River Casino's security room. He'd manually added photos of the Rowland clan to the facial recognition program. He didn't trust Roxanne and trusted her family even less. That slip of the tongue indicating she might be followed could be paranoia, real fear or calculated intent. He leaned toward calculation. She'd certainly played him when she was a teenager.

He almost missed her when she walked in. This was *not* the woman he'd seen in Vegas. Everything about her was toned down—hair, makeup, clothing. He had to look twice to be sure. Then he checked her ID photo. Yes. Same woman. He wondered again who the real Roxanne Rowland was. The ID and the woman waiting at the hostess station in Cyrano's, or the femme fatale in a little black dress and four-inch designer stilettos. Tonight, she wore tight jeans tucked into blinged-out Western boots and a body-hugging sweater belted with leather and silver.

"Keep your eyes open for any of the suspects," Cash ordered the security supervisor.

"Yes, sir. Monitor three is the camera for her table."

Cash's breath came quick and sharp as he watched the hostess escort Roxanne to the table. Concentrating, he leveled out his nerves. This was business. Nothing more. He needed to stay focused. Moments later, a waitress arrived, took her order, then delivered what looked like plain iced tea.

Over the next hour, Roxanne nursed the tea, declined several offers from men and fended off increasingly impatient attentions from the waitress. She became jumpy, staring at the entrance and coming to attention every time someone entered, and constantly checked her watch. Interesting. She looked at her watch a final time, finished the tea and left a tip far larger than the cost of the drink.

Cash smiled, feeling predatory. Showtime.

Roxanne was looking over her shoulder when she plowed into him just outside Cyrano's entrance. Reflex made him grab her arms to steady her, but something far more perverse had him hauling her up against his chest. She held still for a long moment, then pushed her arms between them and attempted to shove him away. He allowed only enough room between them that he could look down into her face.

Those amber eyes of hers widened and she wet her

bottom lip with her tongue. He corralled his libido and pasted a disinterested expression on his face. Snagging her hand, he tugged her along as he returned to the security area. Two uniformed guards waited at the secured door and escorted them to a small interview room. Roxanne's hand tightened convulsively on his as he led her inside. Interesting.

"Have a seat, Ms. Rowland." He held out a chair for her and waited until she sat down before asking, "Why are you here?"

Roxie did her best to curb her panic. She hid her hands under the table, gripping her thighs to control their trembling. Swallowing around the lump clogging her throat, she prayed her voice remained steady. "Why am I here?"

"Easy question, Roxanne."

"No, not really."

"So enlighten me."

Enlighten him? Easy for him to say. She needed to understand what was happening—*why* it was happening—to explain her reasons for contacting him. "Do you have a couple of hours?"

He arched one brow, and darn if that didn't set hummingbirds loose in her stomach. He was just as dark and sexy and…no, not debonair. He was too intense for debonair, too cynical. Cash didn't say anything. He didn't have to. His piercing gaze and that oh-so-eloquent eyebrow spoke volumes.

"You probably don't remember me." Why would he? She'd been a gangly teenager, just turned sixteen, with wild red hair and more than her share of freckles. Mortified, she'd sat in that interview room for almost twenty hours until a fast-talking lawyer in a cheap suit had shown up with the headmistress. Sometimes, Cash had sat across from her, never speaking, just watching. Other times, he'd stood in a corner, shoulder braced against the wall, legs crossed at the ankle and arms either crossed over a very muscular chest or shoved into the front pockets of tailored slacks. Her teenage self had totally fallen for him. Her grown-up self was torn between that remembered hormonal hero worship and total terror.

She huffed out a breath, placing her fisted hands on the table. "My father is a thief." She didn't expect the sharp burst of laughter her statement evoked.

"There's no need to be rude, Mr. Barron." Heat suffused her cheeks but she ignored it. "I didn't have to call you."

"We would have tracked you down eventually."

"I'm not that hard to find."

He slid a hip onto the corner of the table and stared at her. "Last time we sat in a room like this, your name was Anne Landerson."

Her lips pursed at that and she quickly smoothed them out to a hard line as his eyes focused on her mouth. "That's the name I was enrolled with at that school. My father told me it was for security reasons."

Cash laughed again, but this time, the sound was dark and derisive. "Oh, this ought to be good. Spell it out for me, Red."

"Don't call me that."

And there went his eyebrow again. "I…didn't spend much time with my father or brothers growing up. I was left with a family called the Millers until I was old enough for boarding school. I had…" She wondered how to phrase this part. "I was told not use my real name and had a false birth certificate. I had no clue what my father did. I only knew that he traveled, was very dashing and mysterious, and on more than one occasion, I imagined he was an international spy."

His other eyebrow rose, accompanied by a twist at the corner of his mouth. Cash's expression caused her to feel dumb about those childish fantasies. What little girl wanted to believe her father was a criminal?

"On my sixteenth birthday, a box arrived. As I'd never received a gift from my father before, this was a momentous occasion."

"Yeah, I bet."

Ooh. The sarcasm fairly dripped from those three words. "For a girl who had little contact with her family, who had never celebrated birthdays or Christmas, it was."

He shifted off the table, moved to the corner and assumed a posture she'd grown familiar with. Something jiggled his jacket pocket. He reached in and withdrew his cell phone, presumably to send and receive texts. She couldn't keep herself from admiring his long, nimble fingers, even though her blush deepened as her thoughts wandered down completely inappropriate paths.

Cash Barron was fantasy-inducing. Tall, broad-shouldered, with long legs, a slim waist. She could attest to the muscularity of his chest from her stolen moment of weakness earlier that evening. She couldn't help but be struck by the black hair, brown eyes the color of dark-roast coffee and a sculpted face that would make a fashion model jealous. When she'd looked up his bio before calling, Roxie had been shocked to learn he wasn't all that much older than her. At sixteen, she'd been a starry-eyed girl and he'd been very much a man. Confident, handsome, strong. She'd sat there in that room, dreaming about kissing his full lips, about falling into his arms, about... Jerking back from the sexy images, she deep-breathed through a slight panic attack when she discovered him watching her intently. The glint in his eyes was...unsettling.

"So, you received a gift from your mysterious father."

Right back to business. This was good. She should concentrate on business, not...other things. She centered her thoughts. "Yes. I was excited when I opened it. I found what looked like costume jewelry, which I thought odd, given my age and the fact that we'd had little interaction over the years. And then I found the little picture. I thought it was a print—ballerinas in tutus, and I was thrilled. I wanted to be a ballerina at the time, despite the school's dance master rolling his eyes whenever I attempted to dance in toe shoes."

Cash snorted and she glared at him. "I was a lonely girl with no particular talent, Mr. Barron. I was touched because I believed the picture was my father's way of acknowledging my dreams. I didn't read the note attached to the package until later, when it was too late."

"Okay. I'll bite. What did it say?"

And why did her thoughts go right back down that dark road to sexy city? Biting was a big no-no. She cleared her throat. "My father told me to stash the box and keep it safe. I was never meant to open it. It never even occurred to him that I might mistake it for a gift. He didn't remember it was my birthday."

Roxie lifted her head, her gaze colliding with his. "I discovered on my sixteenth birthday that, not only was my father a wanted criminal, but he had so little regard for me that he couldn't be bothered to remember my birthday. As you know, the jewelry turned out to be real and that sweet little print of the ballerinas turned out to be an original Degas, scammed from an eighty-year-old woman by a smooth-talking stranger, according to the police." She dropped her hands to her lap and wiped her sweaty palms on her jeans before continuing. "The next day, I returned to the Millers. I used my birth name after that."

"Want to explain how you ended up here?"

She contemplated that question for a moment. "*Here* here or here in general?"

"In Oklahoma. In Oklahoma City. Why did you go to UCO?"

"Oh. I took online classes and got my GED when I was seventeen. I checked out a directory of American colleges and universities from the library, closed my eyes, opened the book and stabbed my finger on the page."

His dubious expression said it all. "That's the truth, Mr. Barron."

"Why were you in Vegas?"

"I don't really know." She canted her chin at a stubborn angle as her hands gripped the edge of the table. "The itinerary, hotel reservations and boarding pass showed up in my inbox. A weekend jaunt in Vegas, all expenses paid. The email said I'd won a contest. I checked with the airline. The ticket was real so I had no reason to think it was a setup until my brother Brax met me at the airport. I was given a bag of clothes from a high-end boutique, told to—and I quote—doll myself up. On the way down in the elevator, Brax told me I was to…" Her voice faltered and she swallowed down a wave of nausea. "They had a mark. Max was working him on the casino floor. I was supposed to…to be *nice* to him."

"What does that mean?"

She clasped her hands and stared at them, unable to meet Cash's gaze any longer. "They wanted me to get him to his room, to…" She had to swallow again.

"I get the picture." His voice sounded gruff but she still couldn't face him.

"The lights went out and then…"

"And then I almost caught you."

"Yes."

Cash almost believed her—that lonely little girl act was guaranteed to play on a man's protective instincts. If this were a movie, he'd nominate her for an Oscar. She was one terrific actress. The blushes, the swallows, the trembling hands fisted together were all perfect touches.

"Why is your family targeting Barron properties?"

He moved closer, then dropped into the chair across from her.

Roxanne's head jerked up and for a fleeting moment, he wondered if he'd taken her by surprise. A look of consternation quickly followed the one of shock created by his question. Cash had interviewed a lot of people in his life. Instinct insisted this girl was exactly what she seemed—a sweet kid too naive for her own good. But experience persisted in believing her to be as big a con as the rest of her family.

Maximilian Rowland was a consummate thief and scoundrel who had raised his sons in his own mold. Why would such a man not utilize every tool he had—including his beautiful daughter? He shoved the parallel to his own father and brothers to the very back of his mind.

"I…didn't know they were." Her eyebrows pulled into an intriguing vee above the bridge of her scrunched-up nose. She looked cutely perplexed. "I suppose that rather falls in line with why I contacted you."

Leaning back in the chair, he waited for her to continue.

"My father is a…criminal, Mr. Barron. We've been mostly estranged my entire life, but especially since that one incident. My brothers have contacted me periodically, checking up on me, occasionally sending money—which I sent back." She hurried to add that bit of information and again, he almost believed her. "Anyway, the trip to Las Vegas was a complete surprise."

She blinked at him, still portraying her innocence.

"So you had no idea you'd be…" He searched for a word. "*Working* with them?"

"No! None at all. But…" Her voice trailed off and she wouldn't look directly at him.

"But what?"

"I have the feeling they aren't done with me." She leaned forward, her expression earnest. "To be perfectly honest, Mr. Barron, I want nothing to do with them. I like my job. There are things I want to do with my life and they do not include jail time." She inhaled deeply, huffed out the breath and plastered a serious look on her face. "I have a proposal for you."

Cash watched, making sure there was nothing on his face for her to read. "A proposal."

"Yes." She nodded enthusiastically and leaned even closer.

He glanced down, just to see what she was "offering." Nothing. Her sweater remained sedately in place. He was almost disappointed. Then her pursed lips caught his attention.

"You see, as I stated, I don't want anything to do with them, but if you—or the police—can catch them, then I get to keep my life."

"And keeping your life is important to you?"

She tossed him a cute expression meant to convey "duh."

"Exactly. Look, I'm a museum curator by education. I want to work in a museum. Being the corporate archivist for RCM is interesting, but I really want to use my history degree. My father and brothers? They'll ruin everything."

"And your proposal?"

"Oh! I thought I'd said. I'm pretty sure they plan on dragging me into whatever their scheme is. I can pretend to play along, notify you, and you and the police can swoop in and arrest them."

"Swoop in."

She nodded enthusiastically again. "Exactly."

Cash didn't believe her, but he admitted things were getting interesting. "Tell me what you do know."

She rambled along, either filling in blanks or making stuff up as she went. She was an imaginative little thing. He was busy texting Bridger. She had a proposition? He had the beginnings of a plan.

"Um… I still have the dress."

"Dress?" He looked up from his phone.

"Yes, the one I told you about. The one I wore to the casino? It still had the tags when I wore it and I was told not to tear them off because my brother planned to return the dress for credit. Or he shoplifted it and just told me that."

"Uh-huh."

"I want to send it back to the store…or at least find out if someone actually paid for it. I might keep it if Braxton did. He's a pig."

Somewhere along the way, Cash had lost control of the conversation, though the flurry of texts he exchanged with Bridger had been enlightening. According to their account rep at RCM, Roxanne Rowland had been hired as an archivist—basically a glorified librarian charged with cataloging and preserving ad campaign material. They were thrilled to have her, she'd been a model employee, and was there a problem?

He wasn't quite sure when—or why—he made the decision he did, but with one final text, he put his plan into motion.

"Okay, here's the deal. You're moving in with me."

Roxie's face registered shocked denial. "What? No!"

"I don't think you understand, sweetheart. Until this situation is resolved, we're joined at the hip."

"First, I am not your sweetheart."

"Boy, ain't that the truth." He muttered the sentiment under his breath.

"And second, I can't. I have work."

"That's been taken care of. You're on loan to the Barron Companies."

"Wait… I…that can't be! I'm in the middle of a project. You…what in the world will I do for the Barron Companies?"

"The same thing you do for RCM, Red. Bottom line, I'm not letting you out of my sight."

Color tinted her cheeks, and her eyes glinted like bright sun shining on a broken whiskey bottle. "Oh? Really? How does that work, precisely? Are you going to handcuff me to the toilet when you shower? Tie me to the bed?"

"That can be arranged."

Four

Evil. He was just pure evil. Roxie's temper flared even as a wave of unadulterated lust surged through her insides. It had nothing to do with being tied to Cash Barron's bed and everything to do with the man himself. And she needed to murder her girlish fantasies immediately or she'd never survive this debacle intact. She chanced a look in his direction. His expression remained resolute but was that a twinkle of mischief in his eyes?

"Let's go."

"I'm not going anywhere with you. My car is in the parking lot."

"I'll have security drive it home for you."

"I'm perfectly capable of driving myself."

"You're riding with me. We'll go by your apartment, you can pack, then we'll head to my place."

"What part of *no* do you not understand? I have responsibilities. I—" She felt her eyes widen. "I have someone waiting at home for me."

"Who?"

"Um… Harley."

"Who's that?"

Cash's gaze narrowed, and did he sound suspicious or was it something else? Something…intriguing. Like jealousy? Ha. Roxie was just a means to an end. *Jealous* was not a word she would ever associate with Cash. "He's my…roommate." Well, technically speaking, that was true. Harley lived with her. "And I sort of have to take care of him."

Cash leaned closer and peered at her, his gaze sharp and assessing. "What's that mean—you have to take care of him?"

Roxie forced herself to meet his gaze despite the jitters skipping through her. "He's…um…immature. He can't really look after himself."

"Uh-huh."

He totally was not convinced. But there was no way she could leave Harley home alone. "I'm telling the truth, Mr. Barron."

"Uh-huh. C'mon. Let's go meet this guy and see what he has to say about all this."

He latched on to her hand and tugged her along after him. Roxie was suddenly reminded of what walking with Harley was like. She tried to plant her feet, but the leather soles of her boots skidded over the smooth flooring. She attempted to jerk her hand free, but Cash simply tightened his grip and kept walking. She finally gave up and trotted to keep up with his long-legged stride.

When they reached the entrance, there was a dark gray Range Rover waiting, and a man in a black suit, starched white shirt and black tie held the passenger-side door open. He tucked his chin as he extended a hand palm-up and said, "Ma'am, we'll need your keys."

"No, you don't. I'm driving myself home."

The security guard quickly turned his attention to Cash, looking for guidance.

"Give him your keys, Red."

"Gah! No. Get it through your thick head, Mr. Barron. Just because I agreed to help you does not mean you can tell me what to do."

Cash stalked around the vehicle toward her and she stepped back, right into the bulk of the security guard—who didn't give an inch. "Give the nice man your car keys, Roxanne, and get into the Rover."

He glared daggers at her and his mouth was a tight line. This guy definitely meant business. She'd been an idiot to call him. Still, if she ever wanted control of her life back, she needed him. Darn it. She huffed out a breath, dug in her purse and pulled out her key chain.

Cash watched as Roxanne meticulously removed a key from the jumble of metal consisting of more keys, a flashlight, at least ten plastic loyalty tags for various restaurants and stores, and other dangly things like weird jewelry. She passed the key to the guard, then that mess of a key chain disappeared back into the bag hitched over her shoulder.

"Get in the car, Roxanne."

She stuck out her tongue but settled into the front seat. He closed the door and gestured for security to remain there so she couldn't escape. Once he was behind the wheel, he glanced at her.

"Buckle up, buttercup."

Her upper lip curled into a kittenish snarl and he almost laughed. Roxanne Rowland was turning into something totally unexpected. Deep down, Cash wondered if he was getting played. The woman dressed in comfortable clothes and wearing no makeup with a sprinkling of freckles was not the woman he'd watched on the security monitors in Vegas.

The trip from the south end of the metro to the northwest side was made in silence. If she was surprised when they turned into her apartment complex, she didn't show it. He couldn't wait to meet this imaginary roommate. Bridger had checked with the complex's management. Roxanne had a one-bedroom studio and was the only one listed on the lease. If she'd sneaked in a boyfriend, she was in violation.

He parked in a slot near her ground-floor apartment and watched her. She appeared irritated rather than nervous. "Getting out?"

"I was waiting for you to open my door, but you obviously aren't a gentleman." With that, she popped her door open and started to get out—only she was snagged by the seat belt.

Pressing his lips together to keep from laughing, Cash hit the release button to free her. Was she really this klutzy, or was it all an act meant to disarm him? Act or not, she was doing just that.

Stomping up the walkway to her apartment, she inserted her key, pushed the door open and stepped to the side. Cash had about five seconds to prepare for the hairy monster launching in his direction. He braced himself, one foot forward, shoulders lowered, and found his arms full of furry energy intent on slobbering all over his face. He muscled the gigantic dog to the ground and glared at Roxanne. She was doubled over, laughing.

"Thanks for the warning. I'm assuming this is Harley?"

She inhaled deeply and bit her lips for a long moment while she regained her composure. "Yes."

"I'll make arrangements to have him boarded." He recognized his tactical error a second too late. Both woman and dog turned on him.

"Harley is not going to some smelly old kennel! He goes where I go!" The dog barked, an echoing *woof* that rattled windows.

"Oh? What did you do with him while you were in Vegas?" He had her there.

Her face scrunched up into an adorably perplexed expression. "Um… Leo."

"And who is Leo?"

"I'm Leo and girlfriend, you did not tell me you had a date with a fine, *fine* man like this one."

Cash looked up at the man leaning over the balcony above them before returning his attention to Roxanne. "So let Leo take care of him."

"Uh-uh. Not happening. I have company comin' and

I won't have time to be traipsing back and forth to let that creature out every time he thinks he needs to sniff the bushes."

Roxanne turned those golden eyes on him. "Harley suffers from separation anxiety. You're the one who is so insistent I move in with you."

"Whoa! You've really been holdin' out on me, Miss Roxie-anne." If Leo leaned any farther over the railing, the man would fall into the very bushes Harley now sniffed.

As if he knew he was the subject of conversation, the big mutt lumbered over, sat right in front of Cash and put a massive paw on his thigh. The dog *whuffed*, a sound too similar to Roxanne's echoing sigh. He resisted throwing up his arms in surrender.

"Fine, but that thing better be housebroken."

Squaring her shoulders and raising her chin, Roxanne leveled what he supposed was an insulted glare on him. "Good." She turned away and muttered under her breath, "Oh, yeah? I bet you aren't housebroken, Chase Barron."

For the next hour, Cash sat on the couch with the massive furball. The dog sprawled next to him, huge head on his thigh. Roxanne puttered around, packing suitcases and grocery bags full of dog food, toys, brushes and other pet paraphernalia. He was far too amused by her, discovering he was smiling at odd times.

"Okay, I'm ready."

Cash checked her over. Roxanne had tucked her hair up into a messy ponytail and stood in the midst of a pile of stuff. He stared at her, then stared pointedly at the boxes and suitcases around her feet. "Should I call a moving van? We can load up your furniture, too."

"Ha-ha. Not funny. I'm trying to be nice in a difficult situation."

He eyed all the gear. "Nice?"

"Yes. I figured you wouldn't want to be running back and forth between your place and mi—"

Cash's cell rang, cutting her off. He shoved the dog away and stood, phone to his ear. He listened to Bridger without giving away the gist of their conversation, his gaze glued on Roxanne.

"Otto Baer is a whale, according to Tucker. He's never stayed at any of the Barron casinos before the incident with the Rowlands."

He considered that information. A whale, also referred to as a high roller, bet large amounts of money. Casinos offered them lavish "comps," such as free private jet transfers, limousine access and use of the casinos' best suites, to lure them onto the gambling floors.

"What was the deal?" Cash asked the question with careful words.

"That's what's really weird, coz. Tuck checked with Chase and with their concierge. They didn't even know the guy was there."

"Interesting."

"I thought so. He stayed two days, lost some money but not a huge amount, won a little of it back and then took off for Tahoe." Harley bellowed out a bark, and a startled Bridger added, "What the hell was that?"

"One of my new houseguests."

"Do I want to know?"

"Probably not. See what else you can find out. I'm headed to my place as soon as I can get all of Roxanne's stuff loaded in the Rover."

"Roxanne's stuff. Loaded in the Rover. Uh…huh. Care to explain?"

"Executive decision."

"Oh, boy. Can't wait to hear this story. Will I see you at the office in the morning?"

"Yes." Cash clicked off the call before Bridger could ask any further irritating questions. He centered himself and said, "Let's go."

Ignoring the huge wet spot staining his slacks—a splotch that resembled slug slime—he gathered up an armful of boxes and a suitcase. It took them two trips each to stow all of her odds and ends in the cargo area. When it came time to load Harley in the backseat, Cash balked.

"Those are leather seats. Claws and drool do not mix with leather."

Roxanne harrumphed and rolled her eyes. "Fine." She marched back inside and returned quickly with a blanket. "Here, Mr. Fuddy-Duddy."

He was not a fuddy-duddy. He just appreciated fine things, and that included leather seats in his vehicles. "You already owe me a cleaning bill for these slacks. I figured you wouldn't want to add replacement seats to your tab."

"Replacement—" Roxanne's jaw snapped shut and her golden eyes sparked.

Cash had a perverse streak, obviously. Pushing this woman's buttons was far too much fun. He watched her avidly while she bent over, reaching into the vehicle to smooth the blanket over the backseats. He caught a few of her muttered imprecations.

"…made of Corinthian leather…male-chauvinist moron…cheapskate…cars that cost more than some people's houses…hates my dog."

He glanced down at the huge black dog sitting beside him. "Does she always talk to herself?" The animal gazed up with solemn brown eyes and sighed. Cash tilted his head to get a better look at Roxanne's very lovely butt. She backed out of the vehicle and whirled, catching him in the act.

"Really?" she demanded, then muttered, "Add jerk-face to the list."

Biting his lips to stifle a burst of laughter, Cash snapped his fingers at the dog. "Get in the car, mutt."

"He is *not* a mutt. Harley is a full-blooded, pedigreed Newfoundland."

He figured the inside of his mouth would be bloody before they got to his place. "Fine." He snapped his fingers again. "Get in the car, full-blooded, pedigreed Newfoundland mutt."

Harley bounded into the backseat, apparently unconcerned that Cash was dissing him. Roxanne threw her arms up as her anger simmered. She clambered into the front seat and slammed the door. Cash could no longer hold back his laughter. She was cute and feisty and he was far more turned on by that than he should be, given their circumstances. He just managed to choke off his laughter as he got into the driver's seat.

"It's not funny," Roxanne huffed.

"It is from where I'm sitting."

Five

"You have white furniture?" Roxie's voice squeaked. What man in his right mind would have white furniture—white *leather* furniture? Harley took one look at the big couch, jerked so hard she let go of his leash, and leaped. He romped all over it, snuffling, and then finally settled on one end. He sat there as proud as punch.

She glanced over her shoulder. Cash had put down his load and returned to the car for a second one. Snatching the moment of privacy, she waggled her finger at the Newfie. "Harley, get down. Bad dog. Bad, *bad* dog!" The big goof rolled over on his back and offered his belly for rubs. "You are going to cost me a fortune," she groused, but obediently petted the beguiling animal.

"I'll put the damage on your tab."

She whirled to face the other half of her torment.

"It's not my fault that you live in a sterile environment, and I will remind you, *you* are the one who insisted on this arrangement."

His dark brown eyes glinted and she was reminded of dark ale in a glass. "You're laughing at me."

He arched one devilish brow and said, "Am I?"

After nailing him with her most fierce glare, she gestured to the stuff piled in the entry. "Where am I supposed to put all this?"

Roxie could almost see the thoughts whipping through Cash's mind as he glanced down a hallway. She'd bet that way led to danger—in the form of the master bedroom. When she drew her gaze back from that precipice, her eyes collided with his. Her whole body ignited from the half-lidded look and sexy grin he lavished on her. She was far too young for hot flashes, but darn if this man didn't make her want to peel out of her clothes and dance in the sprinklers to cool off.

"Your room—" Cash cleared his throat and she wondered why he'd need to "—is that way." He pointed to an arch next to the kitchen. "Guest bedroom. Attached bath." He pointed to a curtain beyond the open dining room area. "Doors to the patio. There's a little grass. You're responsible for picking up after the dog. The kitchen is tiled. Leave his food and water bowls there. There's a walk-in pantry to store the rest of his stuff."

She nodded at each instruction, half listening while she perused the room. Roxie wasn't quite sure what she'd expected but this condo hadn't even been a faint blip on her radar. Bricktown properties weren't cheap, but this complex? It was one of the most expensive in the area—not that she was surprised. The Barrons were rolling in money. Still, this place was probably the largest unit, with its huge open living room flowing into a high-end chef's kitchen and large dining area.

The floors were hardwood and Harley's nails would leave scratch marks, if not gouges. Rugs were scattered under the furniture. The place looked like the set for an HGTV series. Cash had mentioned that the condo also had outdoor space, and she could just imagine what she'd find out there. The guy probably had a private lap pool. In addition to all the public space, the condo contained at least two bedrooms and baths. And every piece of furniture and artwork was designer unique. That all added up to expensive with a capital *E*.

This man was too rich for her blood. Not that Cash would give her a second look if her family hadn't dragged her into whatever nefarious scheme they were working.

Roxie jumped when Cash touched her chin and closed her gaping mouth. He'd caught her gawking at her surroundings and daydreaming about the man himself. She couldn't afford to lose focus like that. She had to keep her wits about her. Cash Barron did not like her, and had a real issue with her family. Okay, *she* took issue with her family, too, but that was different. They were hers. He was an outsider and he was pushy. A jerk. Aggravating. Exasperating. Sexy. Hot. Smelled like heaven.

"Earth to Roxanne."

"What?" She reacted sharply, embarrassed that she'd floated off again.

"Your dog wants out."

"You can't walk across the room, open *your* door and let him out into *your* backyard?"

"Not my dog, buttercup."

Muttering dark thoughts under her breath, Roxie snapped her fingers and marched over to the curtained door. She had to fumble through yards of material before she found the handles for the French doors hiding behind the draperies. The lock took concentration and more than a little finesse to open. Of course, it would. The man was president of a major security company. This entire place was probably wired for sound and video. She froze.

Harley, impatient to get out, used his 150 pounds to push her out of the way and she grabbed the curtain to keep from falling to the floor. Only the fabric ripped, and the whole wall of material cascaded to the floor, pooling around her where she sat on her tush.

Cash didn't even try to hold in his laughter. All but slapping his knees, he was learning that a person *could* laugh so hard they cried. He had to wipe moisture from his eyes and every time he started to calm down, he'd look at Roxanne, and hilarity once again ensued. Once he convinced himself he was under control, he started across the room to help the girl up.

Harley charged through the back door and must have decided that finding his mistress sitting on the floor was a new game. The giant dog pounced, taking Roxanne down, slobbering all over her face. Her shrieks of protest only incited the mutt to more mayhem. The dog fell off Roxie, tangled his feet in the yards of silk fabric and proceeded to roll up in it.

There'd be no salvaging the curtains and Cash admitted to feeling a sense of relief. The condo had been decorated by one of his father's mistresses and she'd used it as a showroom until Cash came home early from a trip to find her in bed with the guy who'd laid her tile. Glancing around, he discovered the place *was* sterile and stark. The walls were white, the furniture white, the rugs white. The only splashes of color came from the framed art photography on the walls. Most of the prints were black-and-whites but some had odd dashes of red—an umbrella in one rainy-day photo, lips on the pouting female model in another.

He contrasted his space with the one Roxanne had left behind. Her stuff was what some would call shabby chic, or thrift-store vogue. The place looked and felt lived-in—like the houses his older brothers all shared with their wives. Different styles but the same sense of…home.

Jerking his thoughts away from that quagmire, Cash focused on the situation at hand. Roxanne still sat in the floor—either crying or laughing silently. He couldn't tell. He edged around the large granite-topped dining table and stared at his houseguests. Harley pawed at Roxie with both front feet, paddling against her thigh. Her red-rimmed eyes didn't bode well. He clicked his fingers. "Enough, Harley."

The Newf stood up and shook. Hard. Silk curtains and slug slime flew. Cash refused to laugh, though he had to turn around for a long moment to regain his composure. Not that Roxanne noticed. She'd pulled some of the silk over her head.

"Just kill me now, okay?" Her mumbled words elicited a *woof* from Harley, then he danced around her, nosing through the material.

"Harley!" This time he barked out the dog's name and the beast came to sit obediently beside him. Cash glanced down at the woman. She was glaring at the dog. "Need a hand?" he offered.

"No," she snapped at him, pushed the material off and stood. She craned her head to look toward the ceiling where the valance and jalousies had once hung on a brass pole. She heaved a huge sigh. "Let me guess. Real silk, right?"

Cash lifted a negligent shoulder. "Probably."

"Criminy. I'm going to owe you my firstborn at this rate."

Everything stopped for a heartbeat and he stared at her. His rational brain insisted she was simply borrowing a figure of speech to describe her predicament. But that part deep inside he hid from everyone—from his brothers, his twin, even himself—wondered for that brief moment in time what it would be like to hold his child.

"Cash?"

Reality crashed back. "Don't worry about the drapes, Roxanne."

"Um…" She stretched a hesitant hand in his direction. "Are you…okay?"

"I'm fine." Okay, he'd been a little short with her, but whatever. She wasn't his girlfriend. She wasn't his houseguest. She was a suspect in an ongoing investigation. "I'll help carry your junk to the guest room."

He turned on his heel and headed back to the entry hall.

"What about this mess?"

"Leave it." Yeah, definitely short.

"If you say so…" She didn't quite put a period on the end of that sentence.

"I say so. It's late. I have an early morning. That means you do, too."

"Well, all righty then, Mr. Sociable."

With Harley doing his best to trip him, Cash ferried the remainder of Roxanne's belongings to her room. She managed one load, fell over the dog, then wisely waited in the bedroom to direct him where to put the bags, boxes and luggage. After the last load, he paused at the door. He should have said something to her but he wasn't quite sure what.

Cash eventually settled on the tried and true. "Good night, Roxanne."

He shut the door firmly and retreated to the kitchen. Grabbing a beer from the fridge, he headed to the media room. He clicked on the giant-screen TV while waiting for his laptop to power up. He'd catch the OKC Thunder game while checking his email.

After drinking the beer and dealing with a few problems from the office, he was still restless. It was pushing midnight and he needed to sleep. Pausing outside the guest room, he listened at the door. The only sound he caught was a jingling noise—probably the tags on

Harley's collar. The Newf was scratching. Great. He probably had fleas.

He tiptoed away and paused in the kitchen long enough to deposit the beer bottle in the trash. In his bedroom, he stripped down to his boxers and stretched out on his bed in the dark. Cash didn't sleep well on the best of nights. Having others in his space perturbed him more than he wanted to admit. The rhythm was off— different noises, different feel to the atmosphere. He wasn't used to a woman sleeping under his roof.

Two hours later, he was still staring at the ceiling. He got out of bed and wandered out. The living room looked brighter than normal, and he remembered there was no longer a wall of curtains blocking the French doors and windows in the dining area. Security lights and the moon cast a grid pattern across the floor. He couldn't decide if he liked the openness or not. One more thing that was different. And unsettling—as troublesome as the thought of Roxanne sleeping not fifty feet away.

He wasn't hungry or thirsty—not for anything in the refrigerator anyway—so he bypassed the kitchen. The media room was empty. The guest room wasn't. He should have gone back to bed but he didn't. He stood outside the door, breathing shallowly and listening to the indistinct noises on the other side. Two additional sets of breathing sounds—one whispery soft, the other a sonorous snore. Curious, he eased the door open and peeked in.

Roxie lay spread-eagled on her stomach under the sheet and a light blanket. In the low light, her hair created a glowing nimbus against the white pillowcase. The black dog was a dark stain across the foot of the bed. The animal raised his head, snuffled, sighed and dropped back into sleep.

Something knotted up inside Cash but he didn't want to examine the feeling too closely. This woman was getting under his skin and he didn't like that idea—or maybe he liked it *too* much. He closed the door as carefully as he'd opened it and padded barefoot back to his own room. He still felt unsettled but he climbed into bed. After some tossing and turning, he dropped off. Exhausted, he barely noticed the dip of the mattress as a warm body joined him.

Six

Something heavy lay on Cash's chest and hot breath fanned his face. A clammy glob of…something nasty pooled on his bare skin. What the blazes? Something cold and wet nuzzled his face. He pressed his head into his pillow and opened one eye. Big brown eyes, a shiny black nose and trails of slug slime filled his vision.

Harley. The damn dog was gazing at Cash like he was the critter's new best friend—or breakfast. It was hard to tell.

"Get off." The big goof *woofed*, rolled over and burrowed into Cash's side. Laughing despite himself, he shoved the animal off the bed. "Not what I meant."

Cash sat on edge of the mattress and grabbed his watch—all while ignoring the sad-faced dog. Six a.m. It might be Saturday but he had things to do. When Harley shuffled to the door, he figured letting the dog out was probably the first thing on the agenda.

While Harley wandered around sniffing everything in sight inside the enclosed patio, Cash slipped down the hallway. He was more than curious how the dog had gotten out. The door was ajar just enough for a 150-pound dog to amble through. He nudged it with his foot and peered in.

His guest was still sprawled under the sheet, face covered by a web of tousled hair, and she was making soft puffing noises with each exhalation. Roxanne appeared to be dead asleep. Either Harley was Houdini in disguise or Cash hadn't closed the door all the way when he'd spied on the girl earlier.

Ten minutes later, he was doing his best to forget the girl and her dog. Cash had things to do. First up, his daily five-mile run. While he normally used running time to order his thoughts and plan his day, he was failing miserably this morning. Thoughts of tousled auburn hair, golden eyes, pouty lips and an innocence that couldn't be real intruded.

What were her intentions? Why was her family after the Barrons? Where did she fit into the scheme of things? Which Roxanne was the real one—the sexy siren or the adorable klutz? How did he find the answers he needed? The questions beat in his head in time to the thud of his running shoes on the pavement.

The woman was a menace—from her curious offer to help nab her family to his perplexing reaction to her. Especially the latter. He didn't want to think about her as an attractive woman, or the way her skin felt when he touched it. Messy hair should just be messy hair. It shouldn't make him wonder how it would look after a night of hot sex. And he definitely shouldn't be thinking about having sex with the delectable Ms. Rowland. She was nothing more than a grifter, born into the life and raised on the long con.

Wasn't she?

Cash had learned early on to rely on his gut reactions to situations and people. He was seldom wrong. Everything he knew about the Rowlands pointed at Roxanne being smack-dab in the middle of things, right up to her beguiling whiskey-colored eyes.

He pounded the pavement but came no closer to answering the questions circling his brain. And the only answers he had pointed in opposite directions. Roxanne Rowland was an enigma—a woman allegedly raised away from her family, sentenced to boarding schools, whose one brush with the law involved Cash's great-aunt. To cross paths now, six years later? With her father and brothers on the prowl in numerous Barron properties?

In Vegas, the house always held the advantage and the odds. Working security, Cash had learned to watch for the long shot and plan accordingly. That outlier would jump up and bite you in the butt nine times out of ten. So what did that make Roxanne? A puzzle—and one he would solve sooner rather than later. He had no choice. He had a duty to his family to do so, and his father would expect no less from him.

He jerked his thoughts away from his father. He'd molded his life to his father's expectations after his first career lecture. He'd been seven and wanted to join the military like his cousin Hunter Tate. *Barrons aren't soldiers,* his father had said. *They're generals.* As a child, he'd only understood that he'd done something wrong—just as it was wrong when he wanted to join the police force.

Ever since his mother had been killed in a car accident, Cash wanted only to protect his family, wanted to keep them safe from harm. And he'd wanted his father's love and approval. One was just as elusive as the other. As an adult, the need to protect was still strong. Everything he'd done, either at his father's direction or of his own volition, he'd done with that desire in mind.

He wanted his head clear but his thoughts were convoluted this morning. That was the problem. Cons. Questions. Puzzles. Family.

Cash altered his morning routine slightly. He'd programmed the coffeemaker before leaving on his run but on the way back to the condo, he stopped in at Sugarbaker's to pick up breakfast. The place catered to residents in the Deep Deuce/Bricktown area. Part coffee shop with amazing pastries, the store also carried gourmet groceries and takeout for lunch and dinner.

With hot muffins and a few staples, like milk, cream and sugar in tow, he jogged the two blocks to his condo. Harley waited at the door—right where he'd been when Cash left—looking both mournful and miffed. The mutt had attitude and wasn't afraid to show it.

In the kitchen, he found a bleary-eyed Roxanne wearing a thin-strapped camisole and low-riding yoga pants. Cash had never appreciated yoga pants more than he did at that moment. Shifting the grocery bag to hide his reaction, he frowned at her puzzled expression.

"Roxanne?"

She turned to him with a yawn as she bent her arms to her shoulders for a big stretch. A stretch that bared her stomach and gave him a peek at a perfectly formed belly button. Refrigerator. He needed to put the milk and cream in the fridge.

"I need coffee."

"Coffeemaker."

Her gaze slid from him to the machine on the counter. "Coffee?"

She sounded a bit bewildered, and he stifled a laugh by sticking his head in the stainless steel fridge to deposit the perishables. "You get a mug from the cabinet, pick up the carafe, press on the lever and pour."

"Mug?"

He looked at her from behind the fridge door. He pointed to the cabinet above the coffeemaker. "In there." She didn't move. "Roxanne?"

"Yeah?"

"Are you all right?"

"I need coffee." Bewildered tipped over into totally mystified.

"You said that." He stepped closer and she stepped back. Herding her in the opposite direction, he got her around the granite breakfast island and installed on a bar stool. Harley shadowed every step he took.

Roxie plopped her elbows on the cool stone and propped her chin in one palm. Her sleepy eyes tracked every move he made from beneath heavy lids. Snagging two mugs from the cabinet, he glanced over his shoulder. "Black?"

She yawned again, a jaw-cracking widening of her mouth that squinted her eyes shut. "Cream and sugar?"

"Yes." Cash couldn't resist teasing her.

"Huh?"

"Yes, I have cream and sugar. Or milk."

"You drink your coffee with cream and sugar, too?'

"No, I take mine black."

"Then why did you…never mind. Can I have cream and sugar in mine?"

"If you're capable of adding it yourself." He poured coffee into both cups, his to the brim, hers with a little room for additives. Retrieving the carton of cream from the fridge, Cash took pity on Roxie and opened it for her. He placed everything in front of her, including a spoon, before leaning his hips against the counter to watch.

Harley immediately sat in front of him and pawed at Cash's thigh before looking pointedly at the closed pantry door. Did the dog want food? With another swipe of his paw, Harley shuffled to the pantry and stood waiting. Obliging, Cash opened the door and grinned when the mutt grabbed a box of dog bones in his massive muzzle and backed out. Cash took the box and instead pulled out the large rawhide bone he'd also picked up that morning. Harley happily settled on the kitchen floor mouthing the big chewy and leaving a puddle of drool.

Roxie nursed her coffee and savored it like it was a rare vintage wine. "He likes you," she muttered, and Cash caught a hint of jealousy in her tone.

"How long have you had him?"

She finished the coffee in her mug and pushed it toward him with an *Oliver Twist* "more please" look. He snagged the carafe and filled her cup. After she doctored it and took a sip, she answered. "He was a rescue. I think he was two. Maybe three. That was a couple of years ago."

Then Roxie sighed and all but buried her nose in the coffee mug as she gulped the remaining liquid. When it was empty, she held it out a second time.

Cash choked back his laugh and attempted to look serious. "You aren't a morning person, are you?"

Roxie suppressed a snarl but forced her eyes to open wide. She blinked, then stared at Cash, giving the sexy man a long, slow perusal. She took in his broad shoulders, the sculpted chest outlined by a damp cotton T-shirt. Tapered waist, lean hips encased in form-fitting—and, oh, what a form they fitted—running pants that showcased his muscular thighs to perfection.

"And you are, I'm guessing." She dropped her gaze to focus on adding cream and sugar to her coffee.

"I am." The smug amusement in his tone was almost more than she could take this early in the day.

She gulped more of the hot liquid and choked as the sum of his outfit worked through her now caffeine-soaked brain cells. Sputtering, she managed to swallow and not spit out coffee. "Oh my gosh! You run!"

Okay, that came out as an accusation but she didn't care. Runners were…insane. Bordering on evil. Did he do this every day? Would he make her get up and go with him?

"I do." Now he *was* laughing.

A paper towel appeared next to her cup. She wiped her mouth, studiously avoiding looking at Cash, with his lean runner's body that she wanted to press up against and do bad things to. A huge muffin, resting on a small plate with warmth still radiating from it, appeared in her peripheral vision.

"That one is buttermilk spice. If you prefer blueberry or lemon poppy seed, I have those, too."

Buttermilk spice was her favorite muffin in the whole world. It tasted the way she thought family holidays should, not that she had any real idea. Only as an adult, during college and while starting her career, had she any inkling of how normal families—real families—celebrated Thanksgiving and Christmas and…birthdays.

Roxie picked at the edge of the muffin overlapping the paper baking cup. A small piece crumbled into her fingers and she popped it into her mouth. The flavor burst on her tongue—cinnamon, ginger, nutmeg. This might just be the most delicious muffin she'd ever eaten. Peeling back the paper, she picked up the treat and took a real bite. She prevented her eyes from rolling back in her head but she couldn't quite stifle the soft moan of appreciation.

Cash moved, quickly putting the island between them. She lifted her gaze and let out a startled *eep* when she saw his face. His eyes were glued on her and she tried to decipher the look on his face. He edged along the far side of the island and all but dashed across the dining area, his back to her. "I need a shower. Enjoy your muffin and I presume you are now capable of pouring your own coffee?"

"Uh-huh." Her mouth was dry from the quick glimpse she'd caught of him before he turned away. Those muscle-hugging running pants left nothing—*nothing*—to the imagination and oh boy was her imagination doing cartwheels, shaking pompoms, and jumping up and down screaming, "Do me! Do me now!"

No. NononoNO! Roxie reined in her thoughts and concentrated on her muffin. The delicious, her-favorite-kind muffin. Thinking about that man, with that body, naked in the shower? Nope. Not going there. Bad idea. Dangerous road ahead. Slippery when wet. Watch for falling rocks.

Back in control, she finished her muffin and got up to pour one more cup of coffee. She was about to take a drink when Cash stepped out of the door to his bedroom. Wearing. Nothing. But. A. Towel. A towel slung low on his hips. Her fingers stopped working as her brain stuttered to a halt.

Cash held up his cell phone. "There's been a change in plans."

The mug in her hand dropped and shattered on the tile floor.

Seven

Roxanne stared at him, eyes so wide Cash could see the whites circling her irises. Unfazed by the broken crockery, Harley happily slurped up the coffee pooling on the kitchen floor.

"Change in plans?" Did Roxanne just lick her lips?

The towel hitched around his waist stirred. He really needed to get control of his reactions to her. "That's what I said. Harley, stop!" At his sharp order, the dog stopped licking the floor and let out a disgruntled huff. Cash turned his attention to Roxie. "Back out of the kitchen so you don't cut your feet."

She glanced at the floor, as if she'd just realized what had occurred. "Oh. Oops. I'll clean that—"

"You're barefoot. Back out carefully. Go get ready.

We need to hit the road ASAP. I'll clean up the mess as soon as I'm dressed."

Roxie's expression waffled between determination and uncertainty. "Um, where are we going?"

"To the ranch."

Her face lit up and she all but danced over and around the shattered mug. "A ranch? Harley! Did you hear that? We're going to a ranch! Horses! I love horses! We'll have a blast. C'mon!"

The dog barked happily and followed his mistress as she jogged to her room.

Cash stood flat-footed and confused. When had he lost control of this situation? He'd had no intention of taking the blasted dog, but Roxie automatically assumed the mutt would be welcome on this trip. He took a couple of minutes to collect the broken pottery and toss it in the trash. He wet a paper towel to mop up the remaining coffee.

With the sound of the shower splashing from the guest bath, Cash finished cleaning the floor and headed to his bedroom to get dressed. He was on a conference call with two of his agents when Roxie appeared, Harley prancing alongside her.

She had donned well-worn jeans that hugged her in all the right places and Western boots. Her sweater was a color that reminded him of peaches. With the sterile white of his living room as a backdrop, she looked like a ray of sunshine bouncing across a cloud. Her confidence was back in full force. She *looked* like a cowgirl. Walked like one. The ditzy girl was gone and in her place was a lovely woman whose golden eyes glinted with excitement.

He ended the call and prepared for an argument over Harley. He surrendered when he saw the dog sitting next to the door to the garage, leash in his mouth, brown eyes begging. Cash had always been a sucker for big brown eyes.

Once in the Range Rover and headed north on I-35, Roxie broke the silence. "Can I ask how long it'll take to get to this ranch?"

"Since you just asked, I suppose you can."

She huffed a breath and rolled her eyes. "Are you one of those grammar Nazis?"

"Only where you're concerned." He cut his eyes in her direction to judge her reaction.

"Gee, don't I feel special. So, how long?"

"To get to the Crown B? About thirty minutes."

"Oh." She shifted in her seat. "Is there like…a restroom there?" She cleared her throat and added by way of explanation, "I drank a lot of coffee this morning."

He smirked. "Well, we've had indoor plumbing for at least a year or so."

Roxie slapped at his arm. "Do not make me laugh."

"I can pull over and you can find a tree."

"Hardy-har-har. I'm not Harley. I'll wait, thank you very much."

Harley, upon hearing his name, pawed at Cash's shoulder and whined before looking wistfully at the window.

"Fine." Cash hit the button to lower the window just

far enough for the dog to stick his head out, muttering, "Idiot mutt."

Harley, in doggy heaven, nosed into the wind, his ears streaming behind him, along with long ribbons of slime. Cash made a mental note to wash the Rover before the toxic stuff dried and ruined the custom paint job.

Cash should not enjoy sparring with this woman as much as he did. And he should not be working so hard to hide his smiles, because he hadn't smiled this much in months—years, if he were being honest with himself.

Leaning forward, Roxie fiddled with the sound system. She punched through his preset radio stations, apparently dissatisfied with his choices. Admittedly, he had mainly news and sports talk channels programmed, but he also had a few music stations. When she started twisting the knob, he preempted her and pressed the steering wheel controls for the sound system. A moment later, his cousin's voice crooned a ballad.

"Who is that?" Roxie stared intently at the dashboard as if she could divine the identity from the dials.

"Deacon—"

"Tate!" She all but bounced in her seat. Cash should have been used to women reacting this way but it still stung a little. "I *love* Deacon Tate and the Sons of Nashville. I don't recognize this song, though."

"It hasn't been released yet."

"How did you—"

"We run security for Deke's tours, and he's my cousin."

"He's…of course he is. Duh. I remember when Senator Barron announced he was running for president. Deacon played for the crowd."

Roxie settled back into her seat and studied him, her expression serious. "Your family is…wow. You guys really are red-dirt royalty."

He resisted the urge to shrug. Cash hated the term but it was just one more thing to deal with for the privilege of wearing the Barron name. In his business, low-profile was better—a difficult proposition given his identical twin's history of appearing weekly on super-market tabloid front pages.

Exiting the interstate, Cash navigated the country roads to reach the massive rock-and-iron entrance to the Crown B. He followed the meandering drive toward the cluster of homes, ranch buildings and the big house that was the center of the Barron family.

"Oh…wow," Roxie sighed at her first glimpse of the ranch house. "It's gorgeous."

Cash eased on the brake and the Rover rolled to a stop. He looked at the place, trying to see it through fresh eyes.

Roxie continued to gush. "It's…it's like a movie set. A fantasy. This is where you grew up? Oh my gosh, how lucky you and your brothers were to live here!"

Except they hadn't and they weren't. This house had been remodeled, added on, partially rebuilt as it evolved from the functional original ranch house built by his great-grandfather just after the Oklahoma Land Run in 1889. Alice, Cash's dad's first wife and mother of Cash's three oldest brothers, had loved the ranch and remodeled it. Upon her death, Cyrus had moved his sons to a house in Nichols Hills, an exclusive suburb of Oklahoma City.

Cash remembered that house the most, and the touches *his* mother had tried to add before her death. Then it had been Big John and Miz Beth who looked after the house, the ranch and the Barron brothers. As they got older, the ranch had been the place that became home because that's where Big John and Miz Beth lived.

He glanced at Roxie and almost told her that there were no fantasies in that house, no magic in growing up there, but he'd be lying—at least a little bit. He remembered the summer skinny-dips in the cool, spring-fed lake. Fishing on the river. Riding the ranch. Hunting in the fall. The older boys always included the two "stragglers." And they all circled the family wagon whenever Cyrus brought a new stepmother or mistress home.

Shaking off thoughts of his brothers and his father, he drove toward the house again. He was the outsider now and he needed to remember that. It was his job to protect the others, whether they wanted it or not.

Cash kept going rather than pull into the circle drive at the house. He recognized the Ford Explorer parked near the door. Jolie, Cord's wife, was here, which probably meant that his nephew, CJ, was around. The last thing he wanted was for Roxanne to meet any of his sisters-in-law.

He stopped at the ranch's office building. Roxie was unbuckled and out of the Rover before he could kill the engine. She ran-walked to the door and ducked inside. Harley, sensing a chance to escape, vaulted into the front seat and followed her.

Dusty, the Crown B's ranch dog, charged off the porch, barking wildly. Great. The last thing he needed was a dogfight. Harley let out a rumbling *Woof!* Dusty skidded to a halt, almost somersaulting in his haste to stop.

Harley was about twice Dusty's size and Dusty was a big dog—a combination of breeds ranging from sheltie to rottweiler with a bunch of others in the mix. The two critters sniffed each other cautiously, tails stiff but wagging. Then in the mysterious ways of dogs, they became best buds and charged off to explore and mark bushes.

Ranch manager Kaden Waite, and Manuel Sanchez, the ranch's stockman, were waiting in the office when Cash walked in. He glanced around. Both men pointed toward the hall that led to a break room and the bathroom. Roxie hadn't been kidding.

A curvy Latina emerged from the hall, grinned and threw her arms around him. "Yo, Cash. Long time no see."

He couldn't help but smile at the woman while Manuel scowled at him. Manuel had worked on the Crown B for as long as Cash could remember, and the cowboy had raised his family in one of the houses on the property. His oldest daughters, Rosalie and Selena, had taught Cash and his twin, Chase, to French kiss during a particularly steamy game of spin the bottle played up in the hayloft of the big barn.

They'd been caught by Big John. He and his brother had been thirteen. Selena had been the same age and Rosalie two years older. They were lucky Big John found them instead of Manuel. All four of them had been grounded and at the end of the semester, the girls had been transferred to a Catholic school.

Rosalie was now a pediatric nurse practitioner married to a firefighter. Selena had stayed on the ranch, married one of her father's cowboys and now worked for Kade as the ranch secretary. The girls were the closest things to sisters the Barron brothers had.

"How's it going, Leenie? Your cowboy still being sweet to you?"

She threw back her head and laughed. "You know it, *hijo*!" Selena glanced toward the hall. "You been holdin' out on me?"

"What?" It took Cash a minute to figure out she was referring to Roxie. "Ah. No. Business."

"Whatever." Selena didn't sound at all convinced but when her father growled, she backed up, still grinning. "Funny business if you ask me." She waved at her father and her boss. "Yeah, yeah. I'm working."

Kade laughed and patted Manuel on the shoulder before his expression sobered. "We have a problem, Cash."

"So you said." He gazed at the man who might or might not be his half brother. "Explain it to me in detail."

It was Manuel who spoke. "I went out to the north pasture at dawn. We always have a few early calves drop. I found the fence cut. Tracks. They had horses. Took the herd through to the road. Cattle hauler, from the tire tracks I found in the mud."

Cash cut to the bottom line. "How many did we lose?"

"Close to a hundred. All prime heifers ready to calve."

Looking at Kade, Cash waited for the real bottom line. The ranch manager rubbed his hand through his long hair. "Given they were all first years? We're looking at close to seven hundred thousand dollars."

His old man was going to have a cow—figuratively and literally. Cash pulled out his cell, punched in numbers and typed out a text.

"What did you do, Manuel? Step by step."

"I took the Gator out. It has heat. I'm too old for cold mornings on a horse. The herd was scattered. They shouldn't have been. I checked the fence, found the cut. I followed the tracks. I called the sheriff. I called Kade. He called you. And here we are." The older man looked uncertain for a moment. "Should I have called you first, Mr. Cashion?"

Cash shook his head and he, too, clapped Manuel on the shoulder. "Just Cash, Manuel, and you did exactly right. The sheriff's office will get the word out to check all cattle haulers." Dan West had been Oklahoma Highway Patrol before an accident cut his career short. Now he was the newly elected sheriff of Logan County and Cash had the man's cell on speed dial, which he was currently keying in.

"Been waiting for your call," an amused voice answered.

"Seven hundred thousand, Dan."

"Ouch. We put out APBs statewide. Without a description, beyond red mud on the tires and a load of pregnant heifers, we don't have much to go on."

Cash muttered a few words under his breath. "They were slick. I'd bet they have paperwork that looks all nice and legal. I have my team on it. Those cows carry the Crown B brand. Every sale barn within a thousand miles has been put on alert."

The sheriff's laughter rolled from the speaker. "Then why did you drag me out of bed on a Saturday morning?"

"Misery loves company. I owe you a beer. Thanks, man."

"We'll stay on top of things, Cash. And yes, you owe me a beer *and* a burger."

Ending the call, Cash looked up to find Kade and Manuel looking at something behind him. Roxanne. He pivoted and sucked in a breath at the excitement etched on her face.

"Cattle rustlers? Really?" She was all but bouncing up on the tips of her boots. "Are we going to saddle up and go after them? I love riding horses."

Kade smothered a snicker and Manuel cleared his throat. Selena shot Cash a look and mouthed, "Seriously?"

He gave in to the urge and shrugged. "No horses. We'll take the Gator."

"What about Harley?" Roxanne looked around the room.

"What about Harley?"

She waved her hands, her face paling. "Where is Harley? Oh, no. Did you leave him in the car? No, no, no. That's bad. He eats leather seats. I can't afford to replace your seats."

"Breathe, Roxanne. He's not in the car. He got out when you did."

"Got out? Got out!" Her voice rose almost to a screech.

"He's a city dog. He doesn't know anything about the country. About cows or horses or…or…"

"He's with Dusty. He's fine."

Color came back into her cheeks and she breathed deeply several times. Cash did his best to ignore the obvious amusement shared by the room's other occupants.

The office phone buzzed and Selena snagged it before the end of the first ring.

"Crown B Ranch… Miz Beth?… What?… Calm down, Miz Beth, I can't understand—" Selena clapped her hand over her mouth but laughter still escaped. She managed to say, "Cash is here. Talk to him."

Cash grabbed the phone. "Miz Beth?… What?… I… Miz… Fine. We'll come up."

Four people were totally focused on him. "Big John fished Harley out of the pool, but he'd left the back door open."

Roxanne sank onto the nearest chair. "Oh…no." She gazed up at Cash. "Harley's a Newfoundland. A water dog. And his coat…the outer layer…it sort of sheds water unless he's submerged. And when he gets out, he…shakes. A lot."

Well, hell. Cash's chin hit his chest and he rubbed the back of his neck, chasing the knot of tension forming there. Miz Beth was furious. Could this day get any worse?

Eight

Roxanne could still hear the guffaws from the three people in the ranch office. When she'd burst in the door, the two men and one woman had looked up in surprise and she'd asked for the restroom. The woman had pointed and she'd sprinted. She *knew* better than to drink that much coffee before a road trip. But in her defense, she hadn't known there would be a road trip.

Or that Cash would just let Harley run wild. Because the Newf loved water. And could find it faster than an ant could find a picnic. But she hadn't mentioned that to him. Still, what sort of idiot would let a dog out of a car in strange territory and just leave him? Only this wasn't strange territory to Cash and, wait, he'd mentioned someone named Dusty. Had Harley jumped in after this Dusty person had fallen in the pool? The Newfie had a tendency to do that, whether the swimmer needed saving or not. It was instinct.

"Who's Dusty?"

"What?"

Cash seemed distracted and she looked around in time to realize they weren't taking the main drive to the house. He was driving up a gravel road that was little more than a path and headed toward the back of the house.

"Dusty. You said Harley was with Dusty. Is he one of your cowboys or something?"

He cut his eyes her direction. "Or something."

Roxie arched a brow and widened her eyes to indicate she was waiting for the rest of his answer.

"Dusty is our ranch dog."

"A…dog?" Cash had to be the biggest idiot in the world. Who let two strange dogs run off together? To a pool? And some woman named Miz Beth was on the warpath because Harley had gotten out of the pool and run into the house. The main house that was probably as luxurious as everything else the Barrons owned. If she wouldn't strangle herself with the shoulder harness, she'd thunk her head on the dash.

"You've never owned a dog before, have you." She'd meant that to be a question but her sarcastic tone turned it into a statement.

He pulled up before a series of garage doors and parked. "Save the lecture, Red. You have to get in line."

Cash exited the Rover before she could snap her jaw shut. She jumped out and followed him through a wooden gate set in a stone wall and across a landscaped patio with an outdoor kitchen and large pool. She had no time to stop and admire the view as she watched Cash's broad shoulders disappear through a door into the house. She trotted after him and walked into pandemonium.

"That…that beast ate my roast!" An older woman held a rolling pin in one hand and a metal spatula in the other. The front of her apron was soaked and Roxie could see splatters on the cabinets, stainless steel appliances and the tall man standing off to the side. A little boy stood in front of Harley and a large black-and-white dog almost as big as the Newf.

"He didn't mean to, Miz Beth."

The woman shook the spatula at the child. "Don't you be taking up for that monster, CJ, and get away from him. He's foamin' at the mouth. Probably has rabies."

She pushed past Cash to defend her dog. "No, he doesn't. He's a Newfoundland. They…drool. And if he had rabies he wouldn't be dripping all over your kitchen because he'd be afraid of water."

The woman eyed her with hostility. "And who are you?"

"She's with me, Miz Beth." Cash stepped toward them.

The woman turned to glare at him. "Well, that just figures. You owe me a roast and a clean kitchen, Cash Barron." She thrust the kitchen utensils into his hands, shed her apron and waggled a finger at the older man. "Don't you laugh, John Sanders."

"Honey, I just can't help myself. You do make a picture standing there mad as a wet hen."

"That's because I *am* wet, you big galoot. What kind of dog jumps into water in the middle of winter?"

"A Newfoundland bred for water rescue in the North Atlantic," Roxie murmured under her breath.

Miz Beth whirled around to glare at Roxie before returning her attention to the dogs and the little boy. "You get them dogs out of my kitchen, Cordell Joseph. Now scat!"

The kid didn't stick around to argue. He grabbed the black-and-white dog's collar and tried to drag him out. The dog didn't move. Cash whistled, one sharp note.

"Out. Both of you." Cash pointed to the open door. The dogs made a dash for it with the boy hard on their heels.

Roxie was about to ask Miz Beth where the cleaning supplies were kept when the other woman advanced on Cash, stabbing her finger against his chest, eyes narrowed.

"And you, Cashion Matthew Barron. This is all your fault."

Cash backed up a step so Miz Beth couldn't grab his ear. That had been her MO when he was a kid—first the finger and then the ear pinch. Which hurt. A lot. He was settling in to let her tirade run its course when Roxanne waded into the middle of the fray.

"This isn't Cash's fault. Well, not all of it, anyway. Harley is my dog and I insisted we bring him so he could have a day in the country, only I didn't know it would include a pool and a mangy ranch dog—"

"Hey now, Dusty isn't—" Big John began a defense

of the ranch mascot but Roxie rolled right over the top of him.

"And who leaves gates and doors open? You all might live out in the middle of nowhere but there are wild animals out here. What's to keep a herd of coyotes from wandering in and moseying right through that door and stealing your roast?"

Roxanne had her own finger in motion now. Cash took cover with Big John and the two of them wisely let the "women folk" go at it.

"A herd of coyotes? Where are you from, girl? Are you from up north? Dear Lord, we don't need any of your kind around these parts." Miz Beth turned away from Roxie to stare at Cash. "You bring a stranger into my kitchen, Cashion? You've done nothing but stir up trouble and now you bring this…woman and that monster dog of hers—"

"Harley's not a monster! And don't be so hard on Cash. This isn't his fault!" Roxie's cheeks were flushed a becoming pink and her hair almost looked like it was on fire.

Cash glanced at Big John. Yup. He'd caught that flash of triumph in Miz Beth's eyes, too. Miz Beth's reaction to this situation had been totally out of character and now Cash was suspicious of the woman's actions and motive. Then he glimpsed someone attempting to stay out of sight just around the corner in the family room. Jolie, CJ's mom and his brother Cord's wife, her cell phone pressed to her ear as she talked almost as fast as Roxanne.

Crap. He walked on eggshells whenever his sisters-in-law were around. They all pretty much hated him and he believed deep down that his brothers only tolerated his presence because he was the one who kept everyone safe and cleaned up all the family messes.

"You could have handled the situation, Big John." Nodding in Jolie's direction, he didn't keep his disappointment out of his voice. "Roxanne and I didn't have to come up here."

The man who had practically raised the Barron brothers shook his head, but his blue eyes were twinkling. "You have to admit, there's a lot to admire about the way that woman's mind works."

Cash muttered something under his breath that would have gotten his mouth washed out with soap had he been a kid. John guffawed and clapped him on the shoulder. The women, now including Jolie, ignored the men.

"Beth saw you drive around to the office and saw the girl with you. You never brought one out here before. She just wants you to be happy, Cash. She worries about you. We all do."

He glanced sharply at the other man. "What's that supposed to mean?"

Big John's expression turned sad. "Someday, your old man and I are gonna have words, Cash, for what he's done to y'all."

"Leave my father out of this."

Too late, he realized the three women had stopped talking and his declaration dropped into a heavy silence. Fed up, he stomped into the walk-in pantry, grabbed a mop and other supplies. Without a word, he returned to the kitchen and began wiping up the pool water Harley had tracked in. Silently, Roxie took the roll of paper towels and spray cleaner.

When they'd cleaned up the mess the dog had made, Roxie returned the supplies to the pantry while Cash pulled out a money clip. He peeled off a hundred-dollar bill and laid it on the counter. He stared pointedly at Miz Beth while he did it. "To replace the roast."

Roxanne slipped past him and headed for the door. He followed her. On the patio, he whistled sharply. Both dogs came running and CJ stared at him, his mouth forming a little *O*. Cash paused to pet Dusty's head and direct him back to the boy.

"Look after Dusty, will you, CJ? Make sure he doesn't chase the car?"

The child nodded, looking solemn, but didn't speak.

"It'll be okay, bubba. Miz Beth is mad at me, not you."

CJ huffed out a breath as he glanced over his shoulder. "They're all mad at you, Uncle Cash."

"I know. It's okay."

"No, it's not. I know the secret, Uncle Cash. I tried to tell Mom and Dad but they wouldn't listen to me."

Cash didn't breathe for a minute. "There is no secret, CJ."

"Yes, there is. I know why you took me."

Before Cash could react, CJ charged, colliding with his thighs. The boy wrapped his arms around Cash and he wondered when the child had gotten so tall.

CJ leaned his head back so he could look up. Cash obliged by tilting his head down. "Thank you, Uncle

Cash. Without you, I don't think Mom and Dad would be my mommy and daddy."

Before he could respond, the boy turned loose and ran across the yard, yelling for Dusty to follow. Cash didn't speak as he took Roxie's arm and pulled her toward the gate. Even if he knew what to say, he wouldn't be able to get words out around the lump in his throat.

The kid didn't know a damn thing. He hadn't gone with the Oklahoma County deputies to remove CJ from Jolie's home with the plan of getting Jolie and Cord together. He'd been doing his best to break them up, and to secure Cord's rights as CJ's father. That act had been one more nail in the coffin containing his brothers' love. Hell, when it came right down to it, what did a Barron know about love anyway?

Except Cord and Jolie *had* gotten together and married. They now appeared to be living their own happily-ever-after. What a stupid phrase. Except every one of his brothers had found someone who made him happy. And every one of those women was totally wrong for his brothers. His father knew that and Cash knew that. All that happiness made his skin feel tight and itchy. Barron men weren't meant to find true love. Just look at his old man.

His phone rang while he was herding a still-wet Harley into the backseat of the Rover. Speak of the old devil himself. He'd barely said hello before his father started in.

"What are you doing to get my cattle back, boy?"

Yeah, his dad was having that predicted cow about now. "Law enforcement has been alerted. My livestock agents are combing the area sale barns. The fence has been fixed and the remaining cows were moved closer to the home place."

"Who's the woman you moved into your condo?"

That was a question Cash hadn't been expecting but he wasn't surprised his father knew Roxanne was at his place. "She's someone I need to keep an eye on in regard to another situation."

"You turning into your twin now, Cashion? I'm not surprised. I've been waiting for you to betray me just like they did. Disappointment doesn't even come close—"

"I told you, Dad. It's a case. That's all. Look, I have to go. I've got a call coming in. It might be about the cattle." He cut off the call.

After the chewing-out from Miz Beth, Big John's insinuations and now his father's outright accusations, he'd had more family than he could stomach. He climbed into the driver's seat and noticed that Harley seemed unnaturally subdued, as if the dog was picking up on his mood. Backing out of the drive, he glanced at Roxie. She was subdued, too.

Great. Just…great. What a craptastic day and it wasn't even midafternoon. Time to do something different.

Nine

Most Saturday nights, he'd be out somewhere. Either Donovan's, the midtown pub where he usually went, or one of the nightclubs in Bricktown where the party girls hung out looking to hook up. The quiet woman at his side precluded both of those things. For some crazy reason, after that call from his father, he'd driven back to the ranch office and barns and saddled two horses. He'd made the excuse that a trail ride would give Harley time to dry, because who wanted to drive with the stink of wet dog filling the air. Roxanne had all but glowed with excitement and she'd turned out to be a better rider than he'd anticipated. Harley had frisked like a puppy and Cash had sort of felt the same way.

Now they were headed back to Oklahoma City and he had no idea what to do with his guest and her furry

companion. Donovan's didn't seem her kind of place—
not that he had any idea of what she liked to eat or do.
Still, the idea of fish and chips and a Guinness held
appeal.

"How's the furball in public?"

Roxie furrowed her brow. "What do you mean?"

"Do you like fish and chips?"

Her whole face squished into an "I'm totally confused and what was that segue anyway" look. He swallowed his chuckle. "I'm hungry. There's a pub with the
best fish and chips in the state. Can Harley be trusted
to lie under the table and not make trouble?"

"They'd…let him in?" Confusion morphed into
shock before settling into speculation. "Because I happen to love fish and chips."

"Guinness?"

She scrunched her nose. "Harp."

"Close enough."

"Close? Harp is nothing like Guinness."

"Still Irish. Close enough."

Roxie sputtered and looked like she was going to
argue but Harley picked that moment to stick his head
between the seats and bark furiously at the semi-truck
in front of them. The clamor covered Cash's laughter.

An hour later, Harley was installed on the floor of
the back booth at Donovan's, happily gnawing a bone,
Roxie was licking malt vinegar off her fingers, and
Cash thought he was going to lose his mind if she didn't
stop. Her tongue could be a lethal weapon—in more
ways than one. In that moment, Cash knew he would

seduce her. And he would start as soon as he got her back to his place.

She glanced up and sucked in a breath, holding it a moment before exhaling. He studied her from beneath hooded eyes and didn't even try to hide his slow smile as her cheeks flushed. Reaching across the table, Cash snagged her hand and tugged it toward him. He used his own tongue to clean her fingers. The tart, malty taste of the vinegar coupled with the texture of her skin turned his thoughts to tasting her in other places.

"Finished eating?" His voice was little more than a growl.

Roxanne didn't speak, just nodded, as she stared at him with wide eyes. She tugged her bottom lip between her teeth, alternately nibbling and wetting it with the tip of her tongue. He was about three seconds from embarrassing them both. Cash was honest enough to admit that he liked sex. A lot. And he was going to enjoy teaching this woman just how much he liked it.

Tab, dog and woman were handled—one paid, one called, one led by the hand outside to his Rover. Cash helped Roxanne into the passenger seat and leaned across to buckle her seat belt. He enjoyed her quick inhalation almost as much as her exhale. Her breath whispered across his cheek with just enough force to ruffle his hair.

Cash plotted on the way to his condo. Just sex. Roxanne was amenable—as evidenced by the vibes she was putting off. He'd make no promises to her, there would be no flowery words, no declarations of anything more than what this was. Sex. Plain and unadulterated.

Two consenting people attracted to each other, with no commitment.

Perfect. Just the way he liked it.

Twenty minutes later, he had Harley locked out on the patio and was pouring Roxanne a glass of wine. He carried the glass to her, waiting until she'd sipped and swallowed before he moved in. Without touching her with his hands, he leaned forward, his gaze focused on the prize—her lips. A light brush of his against hers, a long pause. Then more pressure and a curious lick with his tongue. She sighed, parting her lips, and that's when he gathered her close, angled her head and kissed her deeply.

Roxie's heart jittered against his chest and it occurred to him that his own drummed out the same erratic beat. This woman definitely turned him on. The calculating part of his brain that never shut off considered the implications. She definitely wasn't his type. In fact, Roxanne Rowland was not a woman he would ever pick out of a crowd, yet he could find her in a sea of faces without a moment's hesitation. The woman he'd watched on security cameras at the Crown Casino was an actress playing a role—poorly, as it turned out. The woman standing here in his living room was a contradiction.

The Roxie he held in his arms was nerdy, a little accident-prone, but seemed…real. She had a temper to match her hair. As clichéd as that was, it was still true. And now it was time to see what else Roxie Rowland was made of. The neck of her sweater was wide, so he eased one side over her shoulder so he could kiss and nibble her skin. She sucked in air and held it. Good. She liked that.

Cash brushed her cheek with his and whispered in her ear. "Drink."

"Are you trying to get me drunk?" Her question came out in a rush of breathless words.

"No. Just relaxed."

A nervous giggle and then, "I don't think I want to be relaxed." Still, she gulped the rest of the wine. While Roxie was doing so, Cash nibbled along her collarbone.

"I love the feel of your skin."

A delicate shiver danced through her and he felt her muscles slacken. Her fingers lost their grip on the wine-glass and it dropped toward the floor. He snatched it in midair.

"Stop doing that."

"Doing what?" He offered a smug grin. "Cleaning up after you?"

"No. Making me lose control."

"Is that what I do to you?" Damn but he hoped so.

Her breathing deepened. "Yes."

Things were progressing right on track. "Good. I think you need to lose control, Red."

"No, I don't. That's not a good thing." She pushed against his chest but the gesture seemed halfhearted.

"I think it's a very good thing."

"Ha. You would. You're a man." Her eyes glittered like whiskey in cut glass. "I think *you* need to lose control."

To prove her point, she wrapped her hands around the back of his neck and tugged his face down to hers.

Balancing on her toes, Roxie stretched up to kiss him. He let her have control for a moment, then claimed her mouth, greedily tasting her with his tongue. It could have been five seconds or five minutes when he finally broke contact. Cash stared down at her, surprised that his breath was hitching in his chest, just as hers was.

"I'm going to make love to you, Roxanne. Sooner or later. Personally, I think it should be now."

Her heavy-lidded eyes ticked up at the corners to match her smile. "That's pretty much sooner, don't you think?"

"Yes."

"Okay."

Cash took her mouth again, holding her tight against him as he walked her backward toward his bedroom. He didn't stop until the backs of her legs bumped up against the mattress. "Last chance, Red."

A languorous sweep of her lashes hid her eyes. When she opened them, he found resolve in her gaze—and longing. Need. Desire. She wanted him. Good, because he wanted her more than— He halted that thought in its tracks. This was just sex. He needed to discover her motivations, what her family's plans were. That's what this seduction was about.

Roxanne reached for the hem of her sweater but he stopped her with a gentle touch. "I'll do that." He trailed a fingertip along the silky skin edged with peach from shoulder to shoulder. "Let me."

"Help yourself." The words sighed out as another shiver danced along her skin, chasing his finger.

Slowly raising the hem, he pulled the sweater off over

her head. Cash forgot about professionalism. He forgot this was just sex, didn't even consider the emotional distance he should keep between them. He forgot about everything but her. Standing there in a lacy pink bra, her skin flushed from his gaze, her lips swollen from his kisses, Roxanne was beautiful. The band holding her hair disappeared with her sweater and dark auburn waves caressed her shoulders.

He gripped her hips, pulled her close and kissed her again. The soft, silky texture of her skin felt incredible beneath his fingers. He could taste the sweetness of the wine splashed with tart, malty vinegar. Just like her: sweet and tart. Her perfume—something subtle with hints of cinnamon and jasmine—went straight to his head.

She twined her arms around his neck, leaned into him. She was… His brain short-circuited. Everything about her—the texture of her skin, her scent, the taste of her lingering on his tongue, the heat surrounding him… She enveloped him. She was everything he could want or need or imagine. His hands found her belt buckle before his brain caught up.

This was a mistake. Taking her, making love to her. No. Sex. This was just sex. She whimpered softly as his knuckles brushed the bare skin of her belly and wanting her morphed into an abiding need. Who was he kidding? This wasn't just sex. He truly wanted to make love to her. As the enemy, she should be forbidden. But that just added an irresistible layer of attraction.

He tugged the buckle apart, undid her jeans, set his teeth on the flesh of her shoulder as he pushed her jeans down her thighs. Her head fell back on a deep sigh and he nibbled his way toward the little moan caught in her throat.

"Something to be said about now," he murmured. Easing her down on the bed, he dropped to his knees to remove her boots, socks and jeans. Then he went back to whisk off her panties. "I'm definitely a here-and-now kinda guy."

"I've heard that about you." She fumbled as her fingers attempted to unbutton his shirt.

Cash leaned back just out of her reach and ripped the shirt over his head without bothering with the buttons. The T-shirt he wore under it disappeared in the next instant. Standing in one smooth motion, he toed off his boots and stripped out of the rest of his clothes.

Roxanne's expression softened. She liked what she saw. Then her gaze sharpened, running over him much like that of an appraiser faced with a piece of fine art. Her tongue appeared, teasing her bottom lip, and his body reacted. That earned him a slow, knowing smile.

"I hope we don't need to call 911," she teased. "I may not survive this."

Bending to snag his jeans, Cash pulled out his cell phone and tossed it on the bed. "You're going to need this."

Her peal of laughter stirred things deep inside him—emotional things he didn't want seeing the light of day.

"Promises, promises."

"Just remember, Red. I never break a promise." He stalked closer and she scooted backward across the bed.

Cash snagged her ankle and tugged her back to the edge. "Did I give you permission to move?"

Her jaw dropped and Cash was delighted to discover that when her temper rose, her entire body flushed. He was pretty sure the sight of her sitting on the side of his bed all pretty and pink was going to keep him company for a very long time.

"My bed, my rules, Red." He lowered to his knees once more and with his hands on her inner thighs, began to spread her legs. He worked slowly, drawing out the process, his eyes locked on her face. When her knees were wide enough to fit his sides, he leaned forward. Only then did he drop his gaze to fully take in the sight of her.

"Beautiful."

Her skin darkened, transforming from pink to a dusky rose. She was embarrassed and Cash found that oddly endearing. Roxie reached for him. One finger traced the line of his jaw, her nail scraping lightly over his five-o'clock shadow. His body tightened in response.

"I should say something," she murmured.

Cash raised a brow but didn't reply.

"Something…memorable or sexy…or something." She sucked in a deep breath and held it as her eyes roamed over him. "But it's really difficult when I don't even have the ability to breathe."

"Give it a shot."

"Wow?"

"That works." He didn't fight the chuckle that followed.

She trailed her fingers down his chest, brushed

through the dark hair there. "No one has ever looked at me like you do."

He furrowed his brow. "Oh?"

"I think I like the way you look at me. At least the way you're looking at me now."

"Then lie back, Red, and let me look my fill."

Roxie shook her head. "No, I don't think so. You want to touch me."

"I do." He enjoyed the way her skin quivered. "I'm going to touch you." He cupped one breast. "Here." His other hand moved lower. "And here."

Roxie's tongue played peekaboo again and he darted forward to catch it with his teeth, giving her bottom lip a little nip in the process. Her eyes closed and she swayed slightly. "You could seduce me with your words alone."

"Where's the fun in that?"

She blinked and studied him, her head tilted slightly. He moved in to kiss the soft spot just under her ear, now that he had easy access.

"What do you see?"

Her question startled him so he leaned back. "What do you mean?"

"When you look at me, like you're looking at me now. What do you see?"

Cash's first thought was to give her a platitude but something in her expression stopped the cliché on the tip of his tongue. He studied her—her apparent wide-eyed innocence, her playfulness, the pouty mouth he wanted to kiss again. "I see a woman who doesn't know who she is."

He could see that his words stunned her, and likely

hurt. He hadn't meant to be that honest, and truth be told, he wasn't sure where the statement had come from.

"I know who I am." She wouldn't meet his gaze.

"No, Red, I don't think you do." He cupped her cheek, urged her gently to look at him. "I see a woman who thinks she knows, but she's just now discovering how amazing she can be."

And where the hell had those words come from? Though he wanted to deny them, he knew them for the truth. "I watch you even when you think I'm not looking."

"That's a little unnerving."

"Maybe. But that's who I am, Roxanne. I study people. It's my job. I can't step away from it. Some people are meant to see others. I'm one of them. And I see you for what you are."

Did he? Wasn't she supposed to be an enemy? Someone he needed to keep an eye on, to protect his family from? But it was him who needed protection. She was burrowing under his skin with her wide-eyed innocence, her expressive face and those damn lips calling to him, demanding he kiss her.

"You don't trust me." She pushed at his shoulders for a fraction of a moment. Then her fingers curled over them and tightened. "You don't trust me," she repeated. "But I don't care." And then she crushed her lips to his.

Cash grabbed what she was offering, tilting her head so he could deepen their kiss. This woman did things to him, sent jolts of excitement sizzling through his system, short-circuiting his brain. He'd started this evening with the intent to seduce her but now found he was the

one being seduced—beguiled by her innocence, her bla-
tant desire. A flood of anticipation washed through him.

He wanted to be reckless, to take something *he*
wanted for a change. To ignore everyone's needs but
this woman's and his own. He wanted to drink her in
with greedy gulps, to live and act only in the moment,
to taste the pleasure and the passion they could share.

When he scooped her into his arms without breaking the kiss, she arched against him, hooking her arms
around his neck. She made needy little whimpers in her
throat and he could feel her pebbled nipples against his
chest. He'd planned to take his time, to taste and tease,
to elicit long, shuddering climaxes from her before finally sinking into her warm depths and giving in to his
own pleasure. Later. There would be time enough later
for that. He wanted her now.

Settling Roxanne on the bed, her head and shoulders cushioned on the pillows piled against the head-
board, he reached blindly for the nightstand drawer. He
didn't want to break the connection between them, but
instead fed at her mouth, caressed her from the slope
of her shoulder to the curve of her hip while he dug out
a condom. Her breathing stuttered when his hand slid
between her thighs. She arched her hips, a husky moan
vibrating against his throat as he found wet heat. A hot
wave of pleasure seared him. All of this was for him.
He had no need to arouse her further. She was ready.

Cash managed to get the package torn open and the
condom on. They were tangled together on the white
comforter, touching, lips searching, in their desperate

struggle to taste, to caress, to somehow get closer than they already were.

Roxanne's magnificent hair splashed across the white pillows like a mass of silken fire. He ran his fingers through it just to see if the waves would burn him. They didn't, but his skin felt scorched anyway. Her scent deepened, grew richer, and he happily filled his lungs with it, drowning in the spicy sweetness.

"Please," she muttered against his mouth. He lost the battle against his greed. He wanted her. The depth of their need would drown them both if he didn't act. His body knew what to do and a moment later, he slid into the wet silk of her center. Propped on his elbows, he looked down at her. Her lips were parted and damp from her tongue. Her skin remained that dusky rose and her nipples puckered, calling his attention to them. He dropped his head and feasted on her. She moved under him, arching her body, her hands on his hips urging him to move with her. He did, with a long, slow withdrawal that left her whimpering.

"More," she demanded.

He surged inside her and she gasped, but her hands clenched him, her nails scored his skin, telling him he was doing it right. He tortured them with another slow retreat. Her muscles clamped around him and he was completely lost. He pounded into her now, rougher than he'd intended, all in a desperate search for more. More of her. More for him. More of them.

His lungs screamed for air and his heart hammered against his ribs. Her skin radiated heat so intense it rivaled the sparks of fire in her hair. He made an effort to gentle his hands but he was ravenous. He'd never get enough of this woman, of Roxanne. He demanded everything from her, he wanted *her*—all of her—now. Right this moment. With a hand cupping the sweet curve of her butt, he changed the angle of his entry. Driving into her, he listened to her gasps, felt the shudders gathering as she arched and opened for him. She cried out, her eyes clouded with passion, topaz replaced by something closer to burnt amber.

Roxanne reached for him blindly, her palms cupping his face before her fingers traced its lines and hollows. Again her nails rasped across his shadow beard and his skin twitched as his muscles tightened in response. She breathed his name, dropping her hands to clutch his shoulders as she drove herself against him, grinding until her inner muscles fisted him, throbbed around him, milked him. He gritted his teeth, continued to pump inside her. "Now, Roxie. Now!"

"Cash!" she rasped. And when she fell apart in his arms, shudders racking her body, he buried his face in the curve of her neck and followed her over the edge.

"Shh, baby. Shhh," he said around his own ragged breathing.

Little aftershocks rocked them both and they clung to each other. Her breath hitched each time one hit and Cash was egotistic enough to enjoy the hell out of the fact that he'd brought her to this state. He raised his head enough to kiss her cheek. When he moved, his sweat-drenched skin glided over hers. She inhaled deeply and sighed.

"Wow," she managed to say after wetting her lips.

"Definitely wow."

She struggled to open her eyes and when she managed to do so, Cash looked into deep pools of sated pleasure. "You certainly are. I think I need the phone now."

"The phone?"

"So I can call 911."

Ten

Cash was laughing—probably at her, but she was too happy and too comfortable to care. His weight on her, the sensation of him still inside her felt…right. She shouldn't go there—shouldn't even stick a toe over that line. His affairs might not make the entertainment news or social pages, but he was a Barron. If his little black book were a digital file, it would probably take up a terabyte of space. He was that darn sexy. He'd melted her bones and they hadn't done anything but the basics. What would he be like— Nope. She was *not* going down that rabbit hole.

"How you doin' down there?"

"Just peachy." His brows quirked and he looked disgruntled. She hurried to add, "I mean that in a very good way. My brain hasn't switched off auxiliary power yet."

That startled another laugh out of him and oh man did that do funny things to her insides. She tightened her thighs and contingent muscles and Cash cut the laugh short. She squeezed again. Did his eyes roll back in his head, and was he getting hard again? How was that even possible? Roxie pressed her head back into the pillows so she could see his face without crossing her eyes. She was about to say something when the bedroom door burst open. She managed a shouted, "Oh, no!" before Harley bounded onto the bed.

The Newf barked happily, licking both of them with abandon. Roxie was trying to fend him off with little success. She was laughing too hard to tell him no. Cash didn't have that problem. He put a muscled arm around the dog's neck and wrestled him to the mattress. They uncoupled in the process and Cash managed to shove the dog onto the floor. He followed with a graceful roll that put him on his feet. Roxie caught a glimpse of his tight butt before he disappeared into the adjoining bath.

As soon as the door closed behind him, Harley was back on the bed, all four feet in the air, tongue lolling from the side of his mouth. She rubbed his belly and choked back her laughter.

"I swear I locked him out in the back."

She hadn't heard Cash leave the bathroom and as she glanced at him, Roxie was disappointed that he'd pulled on a pair of low-riding gym shorts.

"Yeah…about that. I probably should have named

him Houdini. If I'd known about his tendency to escape, I probably would have."

"Why did you name him Harley?"

Feeling a bit sheepish, Roxie tucked her chin against her chest and wrapped her arms around the dog's neck. "Because he's big enough to ride and when he snores, he sounds like a motorcycle."

"He snores." Cash's voice was flat. He closed his eyes. "Great. Just…great."

Sunday had been spent lounging—watching movies, lots of kissing, more than a few sessions of steamy sex followed by steamy showers and an evening topped off with wine, pasta and a bubble bath. But now it was Monday. Normally, she'd be in her office digitizing files, moving boxes, searching for this piece of advertising art or that archived article. Today?

Today, she would be stuck in Cash's office. With Harley. Why Cash insisted the dog come to work was a question she had no answer for. The dog was perfectly happy staying home alone all day snoozing. No one in the building looked a bit surprised when she, Cash and Harley boarded the elevator in the parking garage. They got off on the thirty-fourth floor.

A somber receptionist looked up at the *ding* of the elevator, acknowledged that the big boss was in the house, arched a brow at Roxie and Harley, then answered a phone that might or might not have rung, since Roxie didn't hear a thing. The reception area was backed by a wall of polished black granite. Brass letters, lit from behind, spelled out BARRON SECURITY

SERVICES. Cash didn't say a word as she followed him down a hallway covered with carpet so thick she could see Harley's footprints. At least it wasn't white. She couldn't afford to replace it, either. The thought made her smile. Cash hadn't mentioned her debt lately.

They passed office doors—some closed, some not. Curious faces appeared in the open offices and she could bet that the office grapevine would be humming the moment Cash stepped into his inner sanctum. The rumor mill in her office would definitely be on overtime if she'd walked in first thing on a Monday morning with Cash Barron in tow. The difference was that these people had no clue who she was. At RCM? They *all* knew the Barrons on sight.

At the end of the hall, they entered an open space. A woman of about forty, with stylish dark hair and dressed in a dark pin-striped suit, occupied a huge circular desk that was flanked by matching file cabinets. A space-age-design computer with the largest monitor Roxie had ever seen sat on one end, a telephone system and files cluttered the other. Three doors opened into private offices. One said Bridger Tate, Vice President of Operations. She remembered talking to him on the phone—before Cash had jumped into the conversation. One had no nameplate. The other simply said, Cash Barron. Yeah, no need for titles where the Barrons were concerned.

The woman's expression didn't change as she handed a stack of message slips to Cash. Roxie glanced at her nameplate. Cheryl Carter.

"No fires, Cash. You can work your way through as time allows."

"Thanks, Cheri."

Only then did the woman's gaze flicker to Roxie. "Want me to hold your calls?"

He looked up from reading the top slip and frowned at his administrative assistant. "Why would you do that?"

Cheri raised both eyebrows and tilted her head in Roxie's direction.

Cash glanced from one woman to the other. "Oh. No. Beep me if I need to handle something."

"Of course."

Still riffling through the messages, Cash headed into his office, Harley and Roxie dogging him. At one point, Roxie slipped out to inquire about coffee. Five minutes later, a young man wearing jeans with knife-edge creases and a starched Western shirt appeared with a drink carrier holding two large Styrofoam cups. "Two creams, two sugars," he said as he passed one to her. He set the second cup on Cash's desk.

"Coffeemaker will be installed after lunch, Mr. Barron."

Cash looked up at that and nodded. "Thanks, Nick."

Roxie was about to say something when her phone pinged. She stared at the text on the screen and blanched. Her eyes rose to meet Cash's gaze. She didn't like the way her voice quavered when she announced, "It's Dexter."

Cash was beside her an instant later. She angled her phone so he could see the message, sent all in caps.

WHY AREN'T YOU AT WORK?

She steadied her breathing and willed her thudding heart to slow down to a normal rhythm. "What do I say to him?"

He studied the text before glancing at her. "Tell him the truth. You're working on a special assignment."

She typed out the reply in normal syntax and it had barely been sent when Dex's reply popped up on the screen.

YOU AREN'T IN YOUR OFFICE.

Conscious of Cash's perusal, she typed out, No, I'm on site.

YOU'RE A LIBRARIAN.

Roxie could all but hear the hostility and dismissive tone of her brother's voice in that text. The corner of her mouth curled up in snarl and she narrowed her eyes at her phone. WRONG. I am NOT a librarian. I'm an archivist. There IS a difference. I'm on site curating a client's collection.

I WAITED HOURS FOR YOU IN THE GARAGE.

She eyed Cash as she typed but he already had his phone out and was punching in numbers. Moments later, his door swung open and a man looking very similar to Cash walked in, his own phone glued to his ear. His hair had more russet and his eyes were a clear blue, but the bone structure of their faces was similar.

You're here? Why are you in Oklahoma City?

NOT FOR LONG. CHECKING UP ON YOU BECAUSE YOU NEED TO BE WHERE WE CAN FIND YOU.

Her temper spiked and she typed furiously. Seriously? I have a job, Dexter. A real job. Get lost.

Cash growled at her so she held up a finger. "Just wait. I know my brother."

Thirty seconds later, her phone rang. She tossed a smug I-told-you-so smile in Cash's direction and made sure the man standing next to him saw it, too. She pressed the speakerphone button. "I don't have time to talk to you. Go away."

"Now you listen to me, little girl. This is about family. You ran out on us in Vegas—"

"*I* ran out on *you*? Ha! That's rich. You left me to take the fall, Dexter. Did you tell Max that? I bet you didn't. I bet you told him I got caught and you barely escaped trying to save me."

"That's over and done, Roxanne. You know Max has something big working."

"I know nothing of the sort."

"Well, he does—"

"What, Dex? What does he have working? What are you all dragging me into?"

"It doesn't matter, Rox. We're family. You do as we say, when we say it."

"Oh? Family, are we? So family is all about leaving me hanging like when I was sixteen? I had a blast sitting there in an interrogation room. Just awesome."

"If you hadn't opened the boxes—"

"Whatever, Dexter. I'm not doing this. Tell Max I'm done."

"Doesn't work that way, sister mine. Your last name is Rowland. That puts you in the crosshairs just like the rest of us."

She couldn't breathe for a moment and turned her back on Cash and the other man. "What does that mean, Dex?" She didn't quite manage to keep the quiver out of her voice.

"That means next time you won't have a lawyer show up to bail you out." His voice was muffled by some background noises—or maybe it was the buzzing in her ears. Her hands trembled. "I gotta go. You be where we can find you. One of us will call when you're needed. You come, Roxanne. Or else."

Her phone went dead and Roxie felt as if all the blood had drained from her body. She thought she was breathing but she wasn't sure. She couldn't think. No matter what, her father and brothers would always drag her down into the mud.

"Damn, Cash. And I thought Uncle Cyrus was a piece of work." Cash's colleague scrutinized Roxie before he smiled and extended his hand. "Bridger Tate. And you would be the infamous Roxanne Rowland."

Eleven

Cash was exasperated as texts from his security team filled the screen of his phone. Dexter Rowland had slipped through his fingers again but what infuriated him was the look the jackass had put on Roxanne's face. He'd hurt her feelings and threatened her, but then she got angry and wasn't that a sight to see. Now she was sputtering at Bridger, and Cash inhaled deeply to center his temper and calm down.

"Infamous? Infamous! Are you freaking serious? *Gah!*" She threw her hands in the air and stormed around his office like she was looking for something to pummel.

Harley raised his head, huffed out a growly groan, stretched and thunked his head back on the carpet. If her dog wasn't upset, she must melt down like this periodically. He wisely stayed out of her way and motioned for Bridger to do the same. They retreated to Cash's desk and both of them leaned against the front, their legs stretched in front of them, arms crossed over their chests as she ranted.

"I hate him. I really and truly hate my jerk of a brother. *If I hadn't opened the boxes*..." She managed a fair imitation of her brother's voice. "So that whole mess in Virginia when I was a kid was *my* fault? I can't believe these people. They ignore me all my life and then they think they can just snap their fingers and I'm going to heel? I'm not a dog."

At that word, Harley raised his head again and grumbled.

"No offense, Harley." Seemingly satisfied, the dog lowered his head but now his expressive brown eyes tracked her every move.

So did Cash. Her rant continued, replete with sweeping gestures and voice extremes. He especially enjoyed it when she walked away from him. Her hips swayed in time to her marching stride. He'd always been a butt man. And legs. Hers were curvy and muscular. Breasts were nice, too. He liked the way hers fit the palms of his hands. His fingers curled at the remembered feel of her nipples pressing against his skin.

Bridger cleared his throat and then elbowed Cash. He focused on Roxie. She stood about four feet away, cheeks glowing, eyes sparking, hands fisted on her hips, lips pursed and damn if he didn't want to kiss her. He uncrossed his legs and stood straight in hopes of hiding the evidence of his misdirected thoughts. They had a situation—one that negatively impacted his family and their resources. The last thing Cash should have been doing was standing there mooning over this woman.

"You are such a guy, Cash!"

He blinked, having no real reply for that. He *was* a guy, and being typical of his gender, he replied, "Yeah, and?"

Roxie took two long steps and thumped her fist against his chest. "I know where your mind went. We don't have time for that."

Unable to resist, Cash curled his mouth into a grin and hooded his eyes. "There's always time for *that*, Red."

Coughing now, Bridger backed out of the way. "I think my work here is done."

Cash cut his eyes to his cousin and stopped him with a look. "Actually, she's right. We need to discuss what just happened." He refocused on Roxie, too aware of her closeness and wanting to shift his feet to make adjustments for the increasing discomfort behind his zipper. Duty, he reminded himself, and sidled away to avoid her, ducking behind the relative safety of his desk. Settling in his chair, he scooted forward so he could put his arms on its top and keep everything from the waist down hidden.

Bridger, taking the unspoken hint, dropped into one of the guest chairs. Roxie continued to pace the room. Cash gave her a couple of minutes to calm down. When she didn't, he called her to task.

"Roxie. Sit."

"Sit? I repeat, I am not a dog. I do not come when I'm called—"

Choking back laughter, Cash lifted a brow, giving her an "oh, really?" look.

Flustered, Roxie sputtered a series of incoherent words in protest until she managed, "Shut up, Cash."

He lifted his shoulders in a smug gesture. "The truth is my defense, Red."

"And stop calling me that."

"If the name fits..."

"Argh!"

Cash had set her off again and he watched in amusement as she circled the room in what could pass for a stomp dance. After several circuits she stopped in front of his desk. "Okay, fine. I can tell you have questions. So ask." She dropped into the empty chair and stretched her legs out, her butt perched on the edge.

"You have an interesting way of handling your brother."

Roxie rolled her eyes. "I bet you do, too."

"My brothers aren't the issue here. Yours are. How did you know he'd call you?"

"I didn't. It was a calculated risk. While I don't spend any time with my family, they do drift in and out of my life periodically. And Dex is the next oldest. He's the youngest of the boys." She tilted her head and eyed Cash speculatively. "Just like you. He has a chip on his shoulder. Do you?"

He ignored his instinctual response to the gibe and said, "We aren't talking about me. He wants to prove himself so he acts the major jerk, especially with you."

"If the boot fits," she said under her breath.

Cash didn't appreciate the sentiment. "Stay on target, Roxanne. Why did you try to piss him off?"

"Ha. Shows what you know. I don't have to *try* to piss off my brothers. I do that just by existing, especially Dexter. But knowing what he's like—and knowing he has to get in the last word and be all up in my face about being the boss of me—I knew I'd get him riled if I jerked his chain. You should be happy about this."

Roxie resisted the urge to prop her feet on the front edge of Cash's desk. It was that or fist pump. While she wasn't quite sure how to read his expression, she knew she'd scored some sort of point.

"I should be…happy? Care to explain?"

"Sure. I just guaranteed that they'll include me in whatever they have going on." She had the entire focus of both men, and a small part of her brain curled up. These men were wolves and she was a bunny. Roxie opened her mouth to speak but nothing came out. She cleared her throat and still no words. She gazed at her feet. "Um, can you guys not stare at me like that? It makes me nervous."

She peeked up from under the sheet of hair covering the side of her face. They were exchanging looks. "Hey, not my fault you guys are so scary. For some reason my father wants me involved in this deal. I have no clue why. I have no clue what I'm supposed to do. That whole deal in Vegas? Yeah, that was an unmitigated disaster. I'm still not sure if I was set up to take the fall again. It's not exactly like I was raised in the family business, you know."

"Why do you think they're after the Crown Casino?"

She cut her eyes to Bridger, fully cognizant that Cash's gaze remained fixed on her. Roxie could admit to herself that despite sleeping with Cash—and having the most mind-blowing sex ever—he still intimidated the heck out of her. "Look, you want intel on what they're doing, right?" They nodded and she sat up a little straighter. "Well, since I've spent most of my adult life avoiding their schemes, if I suddenly got all on board with this deal, do you really believe they'd trust me?"

Cash and Bridger exchanged another look. This one she read more clearly.

"So I have to play hard to get. Eventually, they'll need to tell me what's going on. Hopefully, with enough time, you people can be ready to catch them. If not, then I hope you guys can roll with it because we may be improvising out the wazoo."

"We?" Roxie was amazed at how much unhappiness Cash could pack into that one syllable.

"Well, unless one of you two is dressing up in drag, I pretty much need to be there."

Harley picked that moment to stand up, do a downward-dog stretch and start sniffing the furniture. Roxie catapulted out of her chair. "No! Don't you dare, Harley. Bad dog." She snatched the leash on the coffee table near the couch and attempted to hook it to his collar. Harley dodged her and trotted over to lay his head on the arm of Cash's chair. She blew air out with enough force to tousle her side-swept bangs. "Uh, a little help here? He needs to go out. Like now."

Cash ruffled the fur on her dog's head, and checked his watch with a lazy arrogance that grated on her nerves. "We'll break for lunch."

"Roof?" Bridger looked far too nonchalant for Roxie's peace of mind.

A slow smile spread across Cash's face and she almost shivered. The man had devious written all over him.

"What?" She asked the question in her mind out loud and wished she could have called it back. There was clearly something going on.

"Definitely roof. You take Roxie and grab a table. I'll deal with Harley." Cash pushed the Newf away so he could stand. He snapped his fingers and her traitorous dog fell into perfect heeling step with the man.

Roxie turned to the couch to grab her jacket but Bridger shook his head. "You won't need it. We won't be eating on the patio." He took her arm and tugged her toward the door Cash and Harley had just disappeared through.

She and Bridger caught up to man and dog at the elevators. If she hadn't known better, Roxie would have thought Harley was a well-mannered, and obedience-trained, dog. The big double-crosser was sitting next to Cash, his nose all but pressed to the man's hip, as pretty as you please. She curled her lip at the dog to show him she was wise to his shenanigans. The ride up to the fortieth floor was short. When the elevator opened, Bridger led her toward wide mahogany doors while Cash and Harley disappeared around the corner in the opposite direction.

"Where's he taking my dog?" She was so busy looking over her shoulder to catch a glimpse of the two, she tripped and had to grab the back of Bridger's shirt to stay upright.

"Outside."

"On the top floor of a forty-story building?" Okay, she didn't mean to screech it. Not really.

"There's outdoor space that direction. And the restaurant has a patio area they open in nice weather."

"Restaurant? I didn't know there was a restaurant in Barron Tower." She racked her brain trying to remember if any advertising material had crossed her desk.

"It's not open to the public. Only to Barron employees and the building's occupants and clients."

As they reached the massive double doors, one side opened to allow them entry. A rather austere man in a black suit offered a regal nod to Bridger. "Mr. Tate. Will Mr. Barron be joining you for lunch?"

"Yes, Bentley."

"This way, sir."

The maître d' led them to a round table overlooking the city. A girl in a black dress and starched white apron appeared at his elbow with a— Roxie sucked in a breath. The pitcher looked like real silver. The server filled crystal glasses with water and disappeared without a word. Rox was having a hard time reconciling the five-star atmosphere with a restaurant on top of a building in Oklahoma City. New York? Absolutely. Here? Not so much. Oklahomans were more about casual comfort and friendliness than the whole snooty mystique.

There were no menus. According to their waitress, a starched scarecrow of a woman, "Chef" prepared daily specials, each one unique.

"Beef, chicken, pork, fish or vegetarian."

Cash dropped into the chair next to Roxie as Harley crawled under the table. A minute later, the water girl returned carrying a large stainless steel bowl and her silver pitcher. The girl placed the bowl on the floor and filled it. Then, just like before, she disappeared without saying a word. Cash glanced at Roxie. "I know you aren't a vegetarian. She'll have fish. Two beef for me, one rare, one medium rare."

"Beef," Bridger confirmed. "Medium."

The waitress executed a perfect military pivot. Roxie reached for her. "Wait. Excuse me." The woman looked at Roxie's hand on her arm, then lifted her head for a haughty stare. "What sort of fish? What sort of any of these meats? How are they prepared?"

The woman gaped at her as if Roxie had lost what little of her mind was left. "Chef decides. It is always a delightful surprise when his dishes are presented."

For a brief instant, Roxie wondered if Cash and Bridger were pulling a prank on her. The four businessman who were seated nearby made one-word orders to their waiter, so this wasn't a joke. What sort of crazy chef ran this place? She never would have believed that Cash would put up with such nonsense.

"Ahem."

Roxie looked up. She was still touching the waitress.

Oops. She dropped her hand to her lap. "Okay. Fine. Fish. But I'm allergic to tomatoes. And strawberries."

"I'll make note of that, madam."

Madam? Yeah, Roxie might as well crawl under the table and snuggle up with Harley. Before she could carry through with that urge, other patrons turned their attention to the front door as a man entered. Roxie recognized him immediately. The man scanned the room, his gaze stopping on their little group. Cyrus Barron took two long steps and then bellowed, "Cashion!"

Twelve

As the Barron patriarch stormed toward their table, Bridger leaned close to Cash and said, "Please tell me you pooper-scooped after the dog."

Cash, without taking his eyes off his father, muttered out of the corner of his mouth. "Was I supposed to?"

Roxie panicked. In a furious whisper, she hissed, "Please tell me he's not coming over here to yell at me about Harley."

In almost one voice Cash and Bridger said, "He's not coming over here to yell at you about Harley."

"Probably," Cash added.

As if hearing his name was a siren's call, the topic of conversation emerged from beneath the table just as Cyrus Barron arrived. Roxie had moments to grab her napkin and muzzle the beast before he could shake his head. He'd drained the bowl and streamers of slug slime decorated with drops of water trailed from his jowls. She fell out of her chair, napkin flapping, and managed to get one arm around the dog's neck. Too bad she was a fraction of a second too late.

To her horror, the scene unfolded in slow motion like that Tom Hanks movie with the drooly dog. Harley twisted his head from side-to-side, ears and jowls flapping and drool flying. Roxie could almost hear her voice distorted by time slowing down as she dragged out the words, "Ooohhhh noooo." Mr. Barron stepped backward, a look of total disgust on his face. She caught the brunt of the flying slime but a few strands splatted on Mr. Barron's tailored—and probably massively expensive—slacks. She held up her napkin before realizing it was covered in dog goo.

Mr. Barron harrumphed and focused his attention on Cash. Roxie wasn't sure that was a reprieve. "We have things to discuss. Come to my office."

Cash motioned for the waitress, who was carrying a loaded tray, to approach. "After I eat."

"Don't make me come looking for you, boy." Mr. Barron did an about-face and marched out of the restaurant.

Roxie peeked over the edge of the table. Cash was rubbing the center of his forehead with the heel of his palm. She could almost see the headache forming and figured she was probably the cause. She felt awful for creating all the drama. In a muffled voice, she said, "Sorry?"

She caught movement from the corner of her eye—

Bridger getting out of his chair to help her up while the waitress waited for them both to get seated before serving their meals. She shook off his assistance, regaining her composure while she glared at her dog. He didn't look contrite in the least. In fact, he looked pretty darn proud of himself.

The waitress placed two plates in front of Cash. One looked like steak tartare, and the other was a crusted filet served with grilled new potatoes and asparagus spears, drizzled with a creamy white sauce that might be hollandaise, but Roxie suspected it was nothing so "mundane." Bridger also had beef—small medallions braised with a thick, dark roux containing mushrooms, green onions and… She leaned over to get a closer look. Coffee beans? His sides consisted of potatoes, sliced paper thin and layered with Parmesan cheese and butter, and what appeared to be brussels sprouts lightly breaded and sautéed. Her own plate included a lobster tail, grilled and topped with an orange-colored sauce, a nest of julienned potatoes and carrots sprinkled with blue cheese and a side of snow peas.

The silent water girl appeared in the waitress's wake, refilling glasses. Once the serving staff faded away, Cash bent over, snagged Harley's empty bowl and shoveled some all-but-raw meat into it. The dog nosed in and ate with great gusto while the humans sitting nearby watched. Roxie should have felt too embarrassed to eat but her stomach rumbled and the food was too delectable not to enjoy. And she did. Every last bite. If there had been any of the delicious hot yeast rolls left, she would have mopped up the remaining orange sauce on her plate and called it dessert.

As she chewed and swallowed the last bite and reached for her water glass, she looked up. Her gaze collided with Cash's and heat washed through her. He looked like he wanted to eat *her* for dessert. Feeling her skin flush, she swallowed hard and just avoided licking her lips because...company. She could hear Bridger making muffled noises behind his napkin.

When she returned her focus to Cash, he was lounging nonchalantly in his armchair. "Did you enjoy your meal?"

Ooh! He looked so smug and cocky, and she knew exactly what he was thinking. Despite her best efforts, she flushed more and her breathing quickened, because her brain recalled what that man looked like sprawled naked in bed with that same expression on his face. Roxie mentally shook herself. She could not let Cash get under her skin, even though he'd gotten in pretty much everywhere else. He was a player and she was a convenient mark. Once he caught her father and brothers, he'd be done with her. She needed to remember that, especially whenever she got starry-eyed about this whole situation.

As if Cash recognized where her thoughts had turned, he pushed back from the table and stood. "Bridger, take Roxanne back to my office. Cheri can babysit her until I'm done with my father."

Roxanne also stood. "I don't need a babysitter. I'm sure your assistant has far more important work—" She cut off her sentence when she felt the eyes of the other patrons drilling into her back. "We'll discuss this on the way to your office. How much do I owe you for lunch?"

Cash dismissed her question with an insolent wave of his hand. "More than you want to pay, Red."

His cryptic answer stunned her enough that she almost missed Harley, but this time, when the dog stuck his head out from under the table, Roxie managed to snap the leash on his collar *and* wipe his muzzle. She reached within for a false sense of calm and forced a nonchalant expression on her face. Head high, the dog's leash tight in her hand, she followed Cash out, Bridger right behind her.

When Cash kept walking, Bridger very gently circled her biceps with his hand and tugged her to a stop. "We're going down."

"But—"

Cash raised one hand in the air right before he disappeared around the corner.

"He needs to deal with Uncle Cyrus before he can do anything else. C'mon. I'll take you down to Cheri before I get back to work."

She was still arguing with Bridger when the elevator doors opened on the thirty-fourth floor. "Look, I don't need someone—" She clamped her mouth shut as the receptionist's head came up. The woman gave Roxie a steely-eyed stare. Waiting until they were in the common area between Cash's office and Bridger's, she started in once more.

"See? Cheri isn't even here. She's probably at lunch and despite her near-OCD need to keep her desk pristine, I'm betting she's a very busy woman. And you said yourself that you have your own work to do. In fact, I don't even know why I'm here. I could be at my own very busy office doing the work my employer is paying me to do but that isn't getting done because I'm standing here arguing with you about why I can't go back to my apartment, my job and my life."

She paused to take a breath and noticed Bridger staring at her, his expression bemused. "I can tell you aren't from around here originally."

"What's that supposed to mean?"

"It means you said a whole mouthful of things, bouncing from one topic to the one that's really stuck in your craw, all in one breath. I'm amazed, country boy that I am, that I could keep up."

"Har-dee-har-har. You're a real comedian. Why can't I go home?" Bridger frowned so she rushed on, "Or least to my own office. I have projects due, Bridger, and I can't afford to lose my job. Besides, I *like* my job."

"You need to be where we can keep an eye on you."

Roxie blew out an angry breath, counted to ten and worked on putting a patient smile on her face. From Bridger's wry grin, that last ploy didn't work. "Why? Why do you need to keep an eye on me? If you'll remember, I'm the one who called you people. I'm the one who offered to help." Harley tugged against the leash and she dropped it. He wandered over to a leather couch, climbed up and flopped down.

"Let's just say we haven't figured out your long game."

"My long game?" Roxie gave him a hard stare but remembered to keep her mouth closed so she wasn't gaping. "This isn't a game, Bridger. This is my life. I've worked hard to separate from my family. I don't want to be like them."

"So you say."

Bridger stood there, calm, collected, looking perfectly reasonable as he accused her of...dishonesty. Double-dealing. Being untrustworthy. Cash had spent the weekend seducing her and now his top henchman was insinuating that she was...unworthy. Roxie didn't know whether to be angry or hurt.

"Wow." She said the word with no inflection but she was shaking inside. "Guess I know exactly where I stand with you and Cash...er, Mr. Barron. Fine. I'll need to walk Harley soon. Can you arrange for one of your minions to accompany us?"

"I'll have someone come up."

"Awesome." Now she let the sarcasm loose. She moved to the couch and dropped down beside the Newf. The big dog lolled over on his side, his head plopping on her thigh in search of petting. She rubbed his ears, pointedly ignoring the big jerk who was using Cheri's desk phone to call her prison guard to duty.

Roxie sighed and ripped the earbuds from her ears. Three weeks she'd been stuck in this office. Granted, it was bigger than her own, but she had things to do back at RCM. Files to scan, research to be done, items to be preserved and cataloged. Here, she had an empty desk and her cell phone. And a love seat, which Harley currently occupied as he snored contentedly.

She needed to be busy, because idle thoughts? They

led to trouble. The first week had been an adventure—getting to know Cash both publicly and in private. Oh, yeah, especially in private. She'd given up any pretense of believing she was staying in his guest room. Her clothes maybe, but not her. Sleeping with him—and yes that was a euphemism for some very good times between the sheets—was becoming much too necessary to her well-being.

Life had settled into a routine. Cash ran every morning, taking Harley with him. She slept in and was happily awakened to 150 pounds of exuberant dog, 180 pounds of sexy man and something sweet for breakfast. Then they came to the office. Where she spent endless hours being bored to tears—and daydreaming about Cash and all the things she wanted to have with him but couldn't.

She tried to explain her need to stay busy to Cash but he brushed her off. How could a man be so attentive when they were alone and so adamantly stubborn and recalcitrant when it came to her getting back to her job? She'd suggested picking up her work and bringing it to his office. Nope. He even stood there listening whenever she had to call her office to explain things to her assistants.

It wasn't like they'd made headway in the search for her family. The investigation was stalled and every morning, she figured that would be the moment when he said, "We need to talk." And that would be the end of it.

Harley groaned and stretched. It was time for his midafternoon walk. She stuck her head out of her temporary cell. Cheri was talking to the receptionist but Roxie caught the older woman's attention. "It's that time."

"I'll take care of it, hon."

Roxie huffed out a disgruntled sigh. "Tell whoever's coming that I really want to stretch my legs. Harley and I are going to Bricktown to walk the canal."

Ten minutes later, a man in the requisite dark suit knocked on the door. He looked fit, dangerous and highly capable. Which made her want to laugh. She was tied by the leash to a 150-pound dog that ambled. She couldn't outrun Cheri in her stylish suit and elegant pumps, much less a trained security…agent? Guard? Private cop? Whatever. She never knew what to call the parade of men who escorted her on these outings.

"C'mon, Harley. Let's go do your business."

The receptionist was back at her desk as Roxie and her tagalong arrived. The woman looked up from her phone, gave Roxie a spiteful look and then resumed texting as the doors closed, hiding her from sight. They had a straight, express-level ride to the first floor. Still ignoring her escort, Roxie headed out. Harley needed the exercise; she needed away from the tower looming behind her *and* all the people in it, so she set out on the four-block hike to the Bricktown Canal.

She'd just descended from street level to the canal, her shadow trailing her by a few feet, when three women walked toward her. Roxie shortened Harley's leash and scooted over to give them room to pass. They didn't. They stopped right in front of her.

"Miz Beth is right," the brown-haired woman in scrubs said. "He *is* a monster."

The blonde laughed and ruffled Harley's fur. "Naw. Not a monster. A big ol' teddy bear." She bent over to cup Harley's head and croon, "Who's a good boy? You. You're a good boy."

Roxie stood there dumbfounded before realizing that the third woman—a very attractive Native American with gorgeous black hair—remained aloof while giving Roxie the once-over.

"Huh," the raven-haired woman said. "There's no accounting for some people's taste."

Roxie didn't know what she was referring to. "Who the heck are you people?"

The first two laughed, the blonde flashing a wink directed toward the guard at Roxie's back. "I'm Cassidy Barron," she said.

"Jolie Barron." That from the dark-haired nurse.

"Savannah Barron. I'm married to Cash's twin brother."

Roxie backed up a step and bumped into the large man behind her. From the way she spat out Cash's name, there was evidently no love lost between Savannah and her brother-in-law. She wondered what Cash had done to earn that sort of scorn.

"Okay then. Well, nice to sort of bump into you." Roxie tugged on Harley's leash and moved to duck around the women. Two things happened—Harley refused to move and the women stepped forward to cut her off.

"So," Jolie drawled. "You're living with Cash now."

What? Roxie frowned at them. "No. I'm not."

"And he took you to the ranch," Cassidy added. "Several times."

"So?"

She looked at Savannah, waiting for her comment. Savannah just stared back.

"Look, you three might have time for fun and games but I don't. You want to know why I'm staying with Cash, you ask him. Now, if you'll excuse me, I need to walk my dog so I can get back to the Tower of Doom and relieve the Hulk here of his duties."

This time she jerked Harley's leash and he lumbered after her. If she thought she was getting away, she was wrong. The trio fell into step with her.

"So," Cassidy coaxed, "it's been almost a month since you moved in?"

Roxie kept walking, head down, doing her best to ignore them. Knowing Cash and Bridger, they'd probably arranged this little tête-à-tête as way to trap Roxie into revealing something. What, she had no idea.

"I can't believe he'd take her to the ranch," Savannah said from behind her. "In fact, I can't believe he went out there, especially knowing you and CJ were there, Jolie."

Harley stopped, sniffed a bush next to the walkway and did his thing. Roxie pulled a plastic sack out of her messenger bag and cleaned up after him. Still ignoring her entourage, she walked to the nearest trash can and dropped the refuse inside. Pivoting, she headed back the way she'd come.

"Aren't very friendly, are you?" Savannah stood right in front of Roxie, blocking her way.

"Look, I don't know any of you. The three of you swoop down like crows on fresh roadkill and ask questions that are none of your business." She pointed at Savannah. "I get the distinct impression you don't even like Cash, so why do you care what he does, what I do and what we might or might not do together? I repeat, it is none of your business. And your little crack about taste? Yeah, I'm not rich. I'm not gorgeous. But I'm not a bimbo either. Here, I'll make it easy on you. Call your brother-in-law if you want gossip." She glared at Savannah and felt her temper rise. "Now get out of my way."

Harley picked that moment to bark loudly and jerk against the leash. He yanked it out of her hand and bounded down the sidewalk, stopping when he reached the angry man striding toward the group. Cash. And he looked like he wanted to kill Roxie.

Thirteen

Cash wasn't sure who he was mad at. His fingers curled into Harley's ruff while he attempted to regain control. When a text had come in from his security guard Alan, he'd just finished up another round with his father and was feeling the stress. According to the old man, he'd done nothing right in the past month. Despite the lack of incidents. Despite the new security contracts the company had signed. Despite Cash himself doing everything his father demanded.

And now this.

"You know, Roxanne, you look like a nice girl. Why would you hook up with someone like Cash?"

He watched Roxie blanch at Savannah's question, her eyes glued to his face.

"Roxanne." At his voice, his sisters-in-law whirled.

At least Cassidy and Jolie looked a little guilty. Savannah just looked resentful. A part of him understood why they disliked him. Another bit mourned the division between him and his brothers because of his actions against these women. He hadn't even known his twin was in town. But this was his reality. Cash had doubted each one of them and their motives for being with his brothers. And he was still trying to wrap his head around Clay giving up a chance to be president to be with Georgie.

Then there was the part of him that was jealous his siblings had found such happiness. The cynical part kept waiting for shoes to drop and cracks in their relationships to widen and drive them apart. Besides, their father hadn't been a great role model when it came to relationships.

"If you three have questions, ask me, not Roxanne."

"She's living with you and you haven't bothered to introduce her to the family." Cassidy was never one to back down.

"She's staying with me because she's part of an ongoing investigation."

"So…you aren't sleeping together?" Savannah threw him a skeptical look.

"That's hardly your concern, Savannah." Cash stared at each of the three women—catching and holding their gazes for a long moment. "The only thing between Ms. Rowland and me is business. Once the investigation is concluded, she'll be returning to her own residence."

"So the two of you aren't involved?" Jolie looked thoughtful as she asked.

"Beyond the investigation? No. We aren't involved."

Cash caught a glimpse of Roxie but he couldn't read the emotion flitting across her face. Consternation? Misery? She glanced away and a wooden facade settled in its place. Only then did he recognize that he might have hurt her feelings. He'd explain himself later. Right now, he needed to get her away from the wives.

"Look, I know y'all enjoy these little sneak attacks but Roxie is not my girlfriend so leave her out of your schemes."

Cassidy and Jolie exchanged a guilty look and Savannah scuffed the toe of her cowboy boot against the sidewalk. He was just glad that Clay and Georgie were in Washington so he didn't have all four wives ganging up on him. As he watched the women, he saw discomfort morph into alarm as they all looked past him.

He heard three sets of footsteps coming their way, footsteps he recognized.

"Cassie." Chance appeared on Cord's right but didn't approach his wife.

"Oh, hi, darlin'."

Jolie pasted a big smile on her face. "What are you doin' here, Cord?"

Cash glanced at his older brother, who'd halted on his left. "I thought you said you couldn't get away for lunch, Jolie." Was that humor in Cord's voice or was he chiding his wife?

Savannah pasted a stony expression on her face and glared at the man who'd once been Cash's mirror image. After the incident that almost separated his twin and his wife, Cash had started wearing scruff instead of shaving daily.

"Savvie?" Chase brushed past Chance and approached his wife. "Want to explain what's going on?"

Savannah didn't back down. "What? Did *he* call you to come rescue him?"

"No, Cash didn't. So why are y'all here?"

"I'd like the answer to that, too," Chance chimed in.

"I don't know about Cass and Jolie but I wanted to find out what kind of woman would fall for him. We kinda…got a text saying she'd be here," Savannah said.

"We were just curious," Jolie chimed in. "After seeing them at the ranch and then finding out they're living together…"

That caused his brothers to scrutinize *him*. "She's part of my investigation," Cash reiterated. "Those incidents with the hotels and casinos."

"Using that for an excuse again—"

"Enough, Savannah." Chase jumped to Cash's defense, surprising him. "Cash is handling some serious problems that threaten the family business." Chase studied Roxie and that perturbed Cash for some reason he couldn't pinpoint. His twin offered his hand. "Ms. Rowland? You don't look much like the woman I saw on the security cameras. Barron Entertainment appreciates your assistance with this matter."

Roxie pinkened and ducked her chin but she shook Chase's proffered hand. "I just want to help so I can get back to my life."

"Understood." Chase released Roxie's hand and snagged Savannah's. "You and I will talk later, Savvie."

"I still don't know how y'all knew we were here," Cassidy threw in.

Alan cleared his throat. "That would be my doing. After I notified Mr. Barron, I notified your husbands."

Cassidy linked her arm through Chance's and winked at Jolie. "Busted!" She pushed up on the toes of her boots to kiss her husband. "You can't blame us for trying. We were curious about the woman in Cash's life."

"Speak for yourself," Savannah muttered darkly.

Cord snagged Jolie and dropped a kiss on her head. "Don't play matchmaker, sunshine."

"We were concerned, since he'd moved her into his place but hadn't introduced her to anyone." Now his three brothers all exchanged looks and Jolie elbowed Cord in the stomach. "Y'all knew?"

While the three couples devolved into a teasing argument, Cash approached Roxie, Harley's leash in his hand. "C'mon. I'll walk you back to the office."

She executed a precise about-face and marched back the way she'd come without comment. Cash had no trouble matching her stride. They'd climbed the steps to street level and were halfway to Barron Tower before he spoke.

"Don't pay them any mind."

"Why does your twin's wife hate you?"

"She has her reasons."

"That's not an answer."

Resisting the urge to rub the back of his neck, he rolled his shoulders instead. "That's the only answer you're going to get."

"Oh. Because we don't have a relationship. Because

I'm just *business*. Despite the fact I've been sharing your bed for almost a month. Fine. I get it. Shutting up now." She lengthened her stride and pulled away from him.

"Roxie? Roxanne! It's not like that." He caught up to her. "I just said that so they'd leave you alone."

She stopped abruptly and he almost plowed into her. She faced him, her eyes shadowed with misery. "They're your family. Why would you want them to stay away from me? Are you ashamed of me or something?"

Her question caught him flat-footed and she was half a block away before he moved. Tugging Harley into a rolling gallop, Cash ran to catch up.

"Wait, Roxie." He snagged her arm and gently stopped her. "It's not like that."

"Oh. So how is it? Because if it's not those things, it's so much worse."

"Wait...no." He paused to gather his thoughts. "Look, I just wanted to keep you away from them."

"So that's not worse than them leaving me alone?"

"You don't know them."

"You're right. I don't. You never bothered to introduce me, so how could I? And you didn't introduce me because I'm just some...person involved in your investigation who just happens to be warming your bed on a nightly basis. Yeah, I can see why you'd want me separate from your family life."

"I don't have a family life, Roxanne." The bitterness coating those words surprised him. So did the truth of them. "My brothers' wives don't like me. They have reason not to. Anyone I might care about would be fair game for their prying. I didn't want to subject you to that."

"You keep saying they have reason to dislike you. Tell me what you did."

"It doesn't concern you, Roxanne. Just…leave it be. Okay?"

"No, not okay, but whatever." She walked off again and he followed with Harley. Once at the office, they went their separate ways.

She hid out in the spare office and he didn't see her again until the end of the business day. Only he needed to remain at the office for a conference call with a company in Sydney. He tagged Alan to drive Roxie and Harley home and to stay with her until he arrived. He went to the office where he stashed her when he needed privacy and explained. She gathered up her things and leashed Harley without a word.

Cash didn't get home until almost midnight. Alan was on his feet and gave his report immediately as soon as Cash entered the house.

"We had takeout for dinner, which we picked up after the dog's evening walk. She went to bed shortly thereafter and hasn't stirred since."

"Thanks, Alan. I'll see you in the morning."

Locking the door and setting the alarm after the man's departure, Cash didn't put off facing Roxie. He quietly opened the door to his bedroom—and found an empty bed.

"What the—" He jerked off his tie and suit coat, dropping them on the armchair on his side of the bed. Harley met him in the hallway with an aggrieved *woof.*

Cash put the dog out onto the patio and then stalked to the guest room. Roxie didn't belong in the guest room. He should have found her in his bed, where she'd been for—

Cash cut those thoughts off. Given what he'd said that afternoon, her retreat to the guest room shouldn't surprise him, nor should it sting, but it did. He crept into the room and stretched out beside her on the bed. Kissing the back of her neck, he whispered, "Red?"

"Don't call me that."

"Are you still upset?"

"What do you think?"

He curled his arm over her waist and snugged her back against him. "Would it help if I say I'm sorry?"

Roxie rolled to face him and he noticed the circles beneath her eyes. She looked tired. And troubled.

"Will you mean it?"

"I *am* sorry you got dragged into my family drama, Roxie." He realized *he* felt as tired—and as troubled—as she looked.

"Will you tell me about it?"

He considered opening up to her, but twenty years under his father's direct tutelage stopped him. "It's just family, Rox."

"And I'm not family. I get it."

She attempted to roll away but he stopped her by cupping her cheek in his hand. "No, Red, you don't. My family is a hot mess. You don't have anything to do with them, with…things. I can get away from all that when I'm with you."

A tiny smile hovered around the corner of her mouth. "Well, that's a start on the groveling."

"Oh," he teased, his voice growing rougher. "You want groveling." He kissed her and cupped her breast. "My bed is bigger," he hinted.

Roxie was buried under the covers, snug and warm and floating on the last wisps of a dream—a dream of Cash and her living in a beautiful house with little Harleys weaving between their feet. She tripped—klutz that she was—and Cash caught her, laughing as he kissed her.

She'd decided to forgive Cash last night. Yes, he'd hurt her feelings, but the look on his face when he admitted he had problems with his family had almost broken her heart. They were two of a kind in that regard. Her family was no prize, but a little thought niggled at the back of her brain. Cash admitted his sisters-in-law had reason to feel as they did. It was just as obvious that he accepted their dislike and the estrangement it must cause with his brothers as if he expected to be ostracized. That hurt, too.

While she often found him emotionally frustrating, standoffish and cold upon occasion, when he took her into his arms and kissed her? When he made love to her? Her world narrowed and focused, and for the first time in her life, she felt like she might just belong somewhere—belong to someone.

Snuggling back under the covers, she stretched, deliciously stiff and beard-burned in sensitive places. Cash had shown her in so many ways how good he was at *groveling* and, boy, did her body enjoy it. She was about to drop back into sleep when someone started pounding on the door.

Roxie blinked, now fully awake, and sat up. Whoever it was pounded and rang the doorbell like it was a noisemaker on New Year's Eve. Tossing off the covers, she shivered in the cool air and looked around for something to put on. Just because Cash locked himself out when he and Harley went for a run was no excuse to answer the door naked.

A slow smile curled her lips. Maybe that was a good idea after all. If she answered the door naked, maybe Cash would take her back to bed and they'd be a little late to work. Okay, *he'd* be late to work. She'd be late to twiddling her thumbs. With that thought souring her desire, she snagged the shirt Cash had been wearing the night before. He'd dropped it on the chair rather than tossing it in his hamper. Stark white with French cuffs and an impossibly high thread count, she slipped her arms through the shirt's sleeves.

"All right already! I'm coming. Keep your shorts on." She rolled up the sleeves but didn't bother to button the shirt. She turned off the alarm code as Cash had shown her—a guest code he'd delete after she was gone, and wasn't that a depressing thought. When the panel beeped at her, she unlocked and opened the door.

"What? You forgot—" Words dried in her mouth and she scrambled to button up the shirt in the face of Cyrus Barron's disapproval.

The man barged in and pushed past her. She got the door shut but didn't lock it or put the alarm back on as she jogged after him. "Uh…excuse me? Cash isn't here right now—"

"I can see that."

"Well, I'm not sure when he'll—"

Mr. Barron looked her up and down, and his disapproval tipped over into disdain before morphing into outright derision. "I'm surprised my son left one of his bimbos here alone. I thought I taught him better than that. I'll add that to the list of things we need to discuss."

Cash's father stalked toward the kitchen as if he owned the place and once again, Roxie scrambled after him. "Um…" She couldn't say any of the things she was thinking, like "Go away!"

With absolute confidence, he grabbed a mug from the cabinet above the coffeemaker and poured himself a cup. He turned to face her, his eyes as sharp as a hawk's, his mouth pressed into an arrogant sneer. "Cash always did go for the brainless ones."

Brainless? She had a master's in museum studies and was seriously considering going back to school for her PhD. She'd graduated summa cum laude with a 4.0 grade average—for every degree she'd earned. And this dried-up old fart was calling *her* brainless? She bit back what she wanted to say and muzzled her temper. "We've never been introduced, Mr. Barron, and you have no idea who or what I am, and since we've said no more than a few words to each other, I will forgive your natural propensity for antipathy." Then added under her breath, "This time."

The man stared at her like she was something stuck to the bottom of his shoe. Whatever. She'd managed to haphazardly button Cash's shirt so none of her naked bits were showing. She made a mental note to put a robe in Cash's room and start wearing underwear to bed.

Inhaling, she proceeded. "And since you don't know anything about me, I will explain so you understand." She arched a brow. She'd been working on her haughty expression for dealing with her minions—the two interns and three assistants who worked under her supervision in RCM's archives. The old man didn't look impressed so it probably needed more work. Still, she persisted. "My name is Roxanne Rowland and I am the corporate archivist for—"

The front door slammed open and Cash's yelling cut her off. "Dammit, Roxie, what have I told you about leaving the door unlock—" He turned the corner, saw his father, and stopped moving *and* speaking.

Harley, on the other hand, barreled across the living room, hit the tiles in the kitchen and slid sideways as he tried to turn the corner of the kitchen island. With scrabbling claws, the dog kept his feet and his momentum, nailing Mr. Barron with his nose, just below the belt. Roxie never had a chance to stop the collision—not that she was too inclined to try, given the circumstances.

Cash had to shift gears fast. The last person he expected to see standing in his kitchen was his father. The next to last was Roxie, wearing his shirt and nothing else, chewing out his old man. He'd thought the voices he heard from outside were from the TV. And then Harley pulled an end run that all but took his father to the floor. His temples began to throb.

"Ah, Roxanne? Clothes, maybe?"

She glanced down, seemed to realize her state of attire and nodded. "Good idea. And Cash, just so you know…there won't be enough coffee in the world today." She offered his father a scowl before disappearing down the hall to the guest room, calling for Harley to follow.

"What is she doing here, Cashion?"

"Staying in the guest room, Dad."

"Wearing your shirt?"

Cash shrugged. "My sex life has been off the table for discussion since I turned eighteen. Why are you here?"

"I want to know about that phone call you made to Sydney. We discussed this a month ago. I don't want us doing business with those people."

"*We* aren't, Dad. Barron Security is."

"Splitting hairs."

"Am I the CEO of Barron Security?"

"For now."

"Is that a threat?" Something inside Cash tore a little. He'd sat back and watched his father make the same threat to each one of his brothers. They'd all stood up to him, knowing that Chance had them covered under the family trust. Except Cash knew he wasn't protected. There'd been reasons—viable ones—to leave Barron Security outside the trust's umbrella. BSS had clients from around the world and beyond the scope of the Barron umbrella of companies. The company needed autonomy that being in the trust wouldn't provide.

And now he was sweating bullets because the one

thing he could do for his family was shield them through the auspices of his company. If that was taken away? Cash had to face the possibility.

"If it needs to be."

That little rip ruptured, becoming a chasm. He clamped down on his emotions and faced his father. "We'll discuss this at the office. I need to shower and dress."

Cyrus emptied his untouched coffee into the sink and set the mug down with a clink. "You bet we will. And we will be discussing that woman. Get her out of your house, Cashion. Dump her and get your mind back on business." He stopped before getting to the front door. "I'm well aware you've had her stashed in your office, along with that ridiculous dog, and you've taken her to the ranch. That ends now. I know who she is. The Barrons don't associate with trash, boy. You'd better remember that."

Fourteen

Cash should have gone to Roxie, soothed her by telling her everything would be all right, explained that his father often spoke without thinking. Except all of it would be a lie. Nothing was right and his father always said exactly what was on his mind. He heard water running from the bath off the guest room. So much for sharing their morning shower, as they normally did. Harley brushed against his leg and he glanced down. Even the dog looked accusatory.

"What?" he growled. "Dad's right. I shouldn't have gotten involved."

And he was. Very involved. Cash didn't do relationships and, before Roxanne, the thought of a woman sharing his space would have left him laughing. Not that Roxie didn't make him laugh—but in a good way that made him feel warm inside.

Later, when it was time to leave for Barron Tower, Harley refused to get off the couch. No amount of entreaty from Roxie or Cash's commands moved the dog. Frustrated, Cash stormed out of the condo and sat in the Rover until Roxie appeared a few minutes later. As the weather had a tendency to do in early March, winter had come back with a fierce blast of cold. He had the heater cranked up and the seat warmer on high.

Roxie slid into the car, buckled up and never once looked at him. He lasted until they pulled into the parking garage. Leaving the car running for warmth, he twisted to look at her. "You shouldn't have opened the door."

She finally flipped out. "I shouldn't… You… He… I thought… You… What he said…" Then she slugged him. In the shoulder. Harder than he would have given her credit for. "I thought you'd forgotten your keys and it was cold out and you were only wearing those ridiculously sexy running clothes. You are the world's biggest jackass. No. Wait. I apologize to mules everywhere. And I'm wrong. Your father is the biggest. You? You're just…just…" She threw up her hands in frustration. "I'm trash? Is that what you believe? Is that really how you feel?"

Cash grabbed her hands, holding them gently despite her efforts to pull away. "Shh, Red. That's not how I feel. You aren't any of the things my father implied."

She inhaled deeply and quit fighting his grip. "Then why didn't you say something?"

That was a fair question. How did he explain? Could

he explain? How did he summarize twenty-five years of the messy, broken relationship between father and son? "It's…complicated."

"Complicated." Roxie leaned away from him. "Easy excuse, Cash. You don't want to talk about it? Fine." She glanced at the clock in the Rover's dash. "You're late for work."

They exited the vehicle, rode the elevator in silence and he dropped her at the door to the empty office without a word. Yesterday had been rough, though last night's sweet make-up sex had mitigated the situation with his sisters-in-law. Today? Today just made him want to run away. Like to the top of Mount Everest. Instead he was met by a stack of urgent messages.

At 6:00 p.m., Cash emerged from his office for what seemed like the first time all day. Lunch had been delivered to his desk by the ever-present and efficient intern Nick and it felt like his phone was permanently attached to his ear. The niggling headache his morning had started with was now a full-blown head-pounder. Roxie was sitting on the couch across from Cheri's desk, now occupied by Nick, her booted feet propped on the hand-carved wooden coffee table. A part of his tired brain noted that she had a magazine under her feet, probably to keep from marring the polished surface.

"Ready to go home?"

She pulled her earbuds out and studied him. "I've been ready to go home for a month now."

Cash realized his slip immediately but something twinged inside. He'd begun to think…no. He wouldn't go there. He lived in his condo, but it wasn't home, except with Roxie there… No. He couldn't think of that. He studied her the way he would a suspect. Her nonchalance was forced, as was the bored look. He noticed the white-knuckled grip on her phone and the nervous twitch of the toes of one boot.

"You can head out, Nick," he ordered. Once they were alone, Cash sat down beside her, stretched his legs out and planted his boots next to hers. She frowned and he wondered what caused it—him sitting there or his boots on the bare wood. Roxie had funny ideas about furniture and art. He supposed it was her training as a museum curator.

She folded her arms across her chest but refused to look at him. "What?"

"I'm sorry I was too busy to see you today."

Roxie jerked a little and cut her eyes in his direction. He'd taken her by surprise. Good. "And I'm sorry my father dragged you into our family drama."

She didn't respond for almost a minute. "I have no room to talk when it comes to family drama. Mine sort of dragged you into theirs."

He nudged her shoulder with his own in a show of fond solidarity. "How 'bout we head ho—to my place. We'll stop, grab some steaks. I'll grill."

"It's too cold to grill, though Harley would growl at me for saying so. He's a steakaholic."

Cash chuckled. "I'm a man. It's never too cold to grill. C'mon, Red."

He surged to his feet and tugged her up after him. Slinging his arm around her shoulders, he kept her close all the way to his car. The crisis seemed to have passed for the moment.

* * *

Harley, full of prime beef, was sprawled on the couch imitating a dead cockroach, except for the snores that too closely resembled a set of untuned motorcycle pipes. Cash waited for Roxie to step into his bedroom before shutting off the lights in the main part of the condo. He followed her a moment later.

Walking up behind her, he stopped her from taking off her sweater. "I'll do it."

She glanced over her shoulder, her expression concerned. He had sounded gruffer than he'd intended but he needed to be in control tonight. To take charge. To do things his way. Residual resentment from his father's actions lingered, but he refused to allow thoughts of the old man to intrude into his bedroom.

Cash yanked the sweater over her head and tossed it away. As he stroked her bare belly, her silky flesh felt smooth against the calloused tips of his fingers. She shivered beneath his touch and tried to turn in his arms.

"No." He whispered the order against her temple, one arm banding her in place. With his free hand, he captured her wrists and locked them together, his grip firm, unyielding, yet gentle.

"I'm taking you." His voice was clogged with something he didn't want to name. It couldn't be need. He wouldn't let it. "I'm taking you the way I want to."

"I want—"

"No, Red." She struggled a little and he tightened his hold on her. "You'll get what you want. I promise." He unfastened the center hook of her bra and teased the straps off over the points of her shoulders. "But I get what I want first."

At the moment, he wanted her naked. When he dropped his arm to undo her belt buckle and jeans, her bra fluttered open, the straps catching on her elbows. He brushed the hair off the nape of her neck with his chin and nuzzled. He murmured his next command against her skin. "Lose the boots, Red."

"Let me go."

Cash felt his rumbling chuckle all the way through her body. He slid his hand into her jeans, teasing her over her panties. "Boots." He tightened his grip when she twitched.

He scooped her long hair and draped it over one shoulder, kissing his way along her jaw. He captured her chin and turned her head so he could claim her lips, slipping his fingers inside her panties as he did. Teasing her mouth open with his tongue, he did the same with his finger, both plunging into her at the same time. Her body went limp and he swallowed her tiny whimper of need.

Dazed, she leaned against him, tried to toe off one boot, then finally managed and kicked it away. She rubbed against him as she worked on the other boot. He slipped a second finger inside her. She was wet, hot, her sex clamping around him as he stroked her. She shuddered and gasped as a mini-orgasm hit. He didn't give her time to recover, instead urging her forward.

"On the bed, Red. Facedown."

She did as she was told and he stripped her socks and jeans off. Kneeling next to the bed, he rolled her panties down, leaving kisses in the path of their removal. He knelt behind her and spread her knees. Cash intended to take his time, to touch, to taste, to wring every bit of passion from her. When his mouth clamped over her, she erupted.

He held her down on the bed with a forearm across the small of her back. She bucked and writhed, her moans stifled by the thick comforter as she pressed her face against the bed. He feasted on her, tempering his tender assault with kisses along her thighs and cheeks.

Cash glanced up and smiled. Her hands had fisted the comforter and her eyes were squinted shut. Her back heaved with each shuddering breath she sucked in.

"Please," she cried. "Please. I can't. No more."

Heat radiated from her and her skin was tinted rose. He was so hard he had to clench his teeth. He wanted to be inside her so badly he was about to go insane but he held on. He wasn't done with her. "You can. You will."

Cash's fingers filled her, teased her, pumped into her. She could barely breathe, much less speak as his tongue worked her into a frenzy. She begged, sobbing, but still he wouldn't stop. She spiraled higher and higher, and when she shattered, she couldn't control the shaking. A moment later, he was beside her, naked, warm, turning her over and sliding inside.

If she'd had enough breath, Roxie would have screamed from the pleasure of it all. She managed to keep her eyes open, fixed on his face, and what she saw there melted her heart. She'd fallen for Cash, was in-over-her-head in love with him. She clutched him, arching into his body as he made love to her. When she fell the third time, he went with her.

There was a breathless moment of his weight, his warmth, holding her down before he rolled off. He pulled her to him, cuddled her.

"Breathe, Red," he commanded with a pleased chuckle.

She gulped in air, expanded lungs starved for oxygen, found her voice. "Yeah, easy for you to say."

Cash didn't respond and she opened her eyes, tilting her head on his shoulder so she could see his face. He looked infinitely sad and she cringed, the bliss welling inside her popping like gossamer soap bubbles.

Roxie had no pet name for him. No *honey* or *sweetheart*. Nothing as maddeningly endearing as *Red* but calling him by name in this moment seemed…out of sync. Almost harsh. She laughed at herself for even having enough brain cells to rub together after three mind-blowing orgasms. Sliding her cheek against his skin, she curled her fingers through the feathering of dark hair on his chest.

"Thinking too hard, Red."

Cash's voice grumbled beneath her cheek.

"What's wrong?"

"You're the one thinking. I should be asking you that question."

"Worried for you."

"Not worth worrying over."

"Yes, you are."

And that was the root of the problem. Roxie caught

a glimpse of the lonely man he hid from the world before Cash shuttered his expression.

"Cash?"

"I'm fine, Roxanne." He rolled into her, claimed her mouth for a deep kiss, and she knew he was trying to distract her.

When he broke the kiss to nuzzle her breast, she tried again. "What's the deal with your sisters-in-law?"

A low growl emanated from the back of his throat. "I've got your nipple in my mouth and you want to talk about them?"

"Yes. They don't like you much."

"Duh."

"I'd like to know why…and don't give me that family drama excuse. Your brothers came when Alan alerted them to save you from them."

"Hardly. They came to see the show." He sighed and settled on his back, one arm tucked behind his head, his other still curled around her. "Look, Barron men aren't exactly lucky in love. And there were unpleasant circumstances surrounding each of the women my brothers fell for."

"They seem happy enough now."

"Yeah." He stared at the ceiling. "Look, I did the job I was given. I served legal papers on Cassidy. I made sure Cord could claim the son he had with Jolie. I…" Cash closed his eyes. "I tried to save Clay from living through the illness and death of another woman he loved."

"Another?"

"His mother, when he was a kid. Then Georgie."

"But Georgie didn't die."

"I underestimated her strength. And his."

"And Chase?"

"No."

"His wife really dislikes you."

"Yeah."

She stroked her fingers along the dips and curves of his chest and abdomen, continuing even when he spoke again. "They...when they got married, they didn't love each other."

"How could you know that?"

"They'd known each other for all of forty-eight hours when they eloped."

Something in his voice alerted her to more underlying currents. "Do you feel...left out?"

Cash glanced at her sharply. "Why should I?"

"I have the impression that the five of you used to hang around together. A lot."

"Clay is twelve years older. We never hung around. And he's been in Washington for years. Chance is six years older, Cord eight. We didn't hang with them either."

"Maybe not as kids, but as adults. I mean, you all work in the same building. Well, except Clay. Surely you did lunch occasionally or went out for happy hour? And there had to be times at the ranch—" The expression on his face dried her mouth up and no more words came. As quickly as she stopped speaking, he shut down, his eyes glinting with cynicism, those full lips that could work such magic on her pressed into a hard line.

"Leave it be, Roxie. You can't change things. They

are what they are." He kissed her forehead, to take the sting out of his harsh tone, she suspected.

She raised her face to his and claimed a real kiss before murmuring, "Tomorrow is another day."

Fifteen

Cash was exhausted. He'd had meetings with his father every day this week. They'd recovered half the stolen cattle, and a situation at one of the hotels in Florida had been resolved without a lawsuit thanks to his investigators, but there was still no sign of the freaking Rowlands. Today, he'd dodged a bullet; his father had gone off on some tangent that didn't involve him. Still, every meeting had ended with the same question, "Have you gotten rid of that woman yet?"

And he'd stalled. He told himself he didn't need Roxie in his life. Part of him didn't want her there, yet there she was, day in and day out. And nights in his bed, even if he was too worn out from stress to do anything but hold her while he slept. She was always just…there. Smiling. Occasionally making him laugh. Always ready for his kisses—and more. Since he was being honest, he also liked having her big, goofy dog underfoot, too.

He paused in the lobby to send Roxie a text.

Meet me in my office. Two stops to make, then we'll sneak out early.

They'd go home, change and then he'd take her to Donovan's. He thought Roxie would enjoy listening to the Irish folk group slated to perform there. With April almost here, the weather had turned mild and the band would be playing on the patio, so Harley would be comfortable.

Cash got off the elevator at the thirty-sixth floor and dropped a file off at the reception desk for Barron Exploration. There'd been a situation involving embezzlement by a BarEx employee. The file held the evidence of the investigation Cash had run. Next stop, Barron & Associates to drop off a copy for Chance.

He didn't bother waiting for the elevator, opting for the stairs since he was headed down only two floors. Pushing through the fire door, he all but knocked Nick down.

"Hey, boss!" The kid grinned at him while glancing at the file. "If you need to deliver that, I can take it."

"Yeah, thanks." He passed off the paperwork and headed back to the elevator. Cash felt wound up tight, and he very much wanted to get out of his corporate skin to spend time with Roxie. The elevator opened and as soon as he saw his father, he knew all bets were off.

"Cashion."

He resisted the urge to slump his shoulders in defeat. Posture stiff, he stepped into the elevator. "Not here, Dad. My office."

Cheri looked up as they walked in and her smile faded. Then his assistant's face twitched as an elaborate and unreadable set of expressions danced across her face. He didn't have time to decipher them today. He wanted to get rid of his father, grab Roxie and get the hell away from the office. He pushed his door open and led the way into his inner sanctum, closing the door behind his dad.

"I'm tired of waiting, Cashion."

"For what, Dad?" He did his best not to sound as tired as he felt.

"For you to get rid of that woman. She's still in your house."

"My private life isn't up for discussion."

"When it involves women like her, it does. How much are those criminals costing us?"

"I'm on top of the investigation, Dad. Let me do the job you hired me for."

"And that's the operative word, isn't it? Or have you forgotten I'm the one who signs your paycheck?"

"Kinda hard to do that when you're in my face reminding me every five minutes." Cash wanted to retract those words the second they left his mouth.

"I expected better of you, Cashion. The older boys were too coddled by their mother. And Chasen was too erratic. I put all my hope in you, boy. You were to be my legacy. My one true son. And look what you're doing to me."

"What, Dad? What am I doing to you?" The beast that was his temper had escaped its cage. "I'm doing exactly what you ask of me. No matter the damn consequences. I've done everything in my power to protect this family, to make sure our companies run smoothly, to make sure no one can mess with us."

"But that woman is still in your bed."

"So what, Dad? How many bimbos have you bedded for the sex? Because that's what this is. Roxie is the key to prosecuting her family and if she wants to put out while we wait for the next move, how is that any different from the women who warm your bed?"

He headed toward his desk, then faltered. The snow globe that normally occupied a spot near the one photo he allowed in his office was missing. His gaze swept the desktop. The framed photo, of the Barron brothers sitting on a fence at the ranch at Christmastime, was untouched. He and Chase had been eight the year they received antique snow globes from their mother, two weeks before she was killed by a drunk driver.

"Are you listening to me, boy?" Cyrus grabbed his arm, spun Cash around. "I've had all of the foolishness I can stomach. It's time to get rid of her and move on. I need your full attention. I've written off your brothers but I expect you to live up to your obligations."

His father stalked to the door and pushed it open. "I'm disappointed in you, boy."

Cash followed him out into the private reception area. At least Cheri was nowhere to be seen, so no one would see his fall from grace. It was all he could do to maintain his equilibrium. He'd built his whole life around pleasing this man, around getting his respect and acceptance. And now his father was threatening to rip it all away because he'd allowed his desire for a woman to overshadow his duty. He should have known better.

"Get rid of her, Cashion, or you will both be sorry. You know what I'm capable of."

Cash stood stock-still, a burning ache knotting his stomach. He knew exactly what his father was capable of. Remaining outwardly calm, he said, "Why are you threatening me, Dad?"

Cyrus stepped up to him, circled. Cash turned to keep his father in front of him until Cash's back was to the open office door.

"You were my protégé, the one I spent years grooming. And now you betray me. Over some woman. You're no better than *them*." Cyrus waved a hand in the direction behind Cash before he pushed past and stormed away.

A hand landed on Cash's shoulder. "Welcome to the club, bro."

He shook off his twin's grip and faced his brothers. Why were all of them here? Clay stayed in Washington and Chase traveled constantly. Though Cord and Chance occupied their offices on a daily basis, Cash didn't often interact with them, hadn't since they'd married. Each of his brothers wore an expression of pity. Pity for him. "Screw you, Chase."

Cash didn't need this BS. He'd always put the family first, done what was right for the Barron name. He reminded himself that Roxie was only in his life because of a threat to the family. And it wasn't like anything was going on between them. Besides the sex. Which was, admittedly, some of the best he'd ever had. But she was just a means to an end. He didn't have feelings for her. None. She was simply a distraction, like his father insisted. He didn't want her. Certainly didn't need her.

In fact, he couldn't wait to move her and that damn slobbering beast of hers out of his condo. He wanted life returned to normal—ordered, calm, collected. No more lacy bras hanging in his bathroom. No slug slime on his tailored slacks. No muddy footprints on the leather seats in his Range Rover. No more sexy woman sharing his bed.

Chase threw his head back and laughed. "Yup, dazed and confused. She must be some kind of woman to make the last Barron brother bite the dust."

"You aren't nearly as funny as you think you are." Cash glared at his brothers. "Some reason all of you are hanging around here? If you're just waiting for Dad to hand my ass to me again, too late. Show's over and you can get on back to your lives."

He stormed into his office and jerked the door shut, ignoring the soft protests he left in his wake. Cash had more important things to do—like get rid of a woman he should never have been involved with.

Sixteen

Roxie managed to keep her breathing controlled and quiet. Ducking under Chase's desk had been a monumental mistake, especially since his father had followed him in and shut the door. Their argument raged over her head and she hadn't missed a word. The same with the confrontation Cash had with his brothers. When the door slammed, she remained in hiding, her heart hammering in her chest.

The fact that it was still beating surprised the heck out of her. The things Cord said didn't break her, they shredded her. And made her angry. She was such a fool.

"You can come out now, Roxanne." Cash's voice sounded flat.

She crawled out from the kneehole and used his luxurious leather desk chair as a prop to climb to her feet.

Facing the windows, her back to the room, she did not want to turn around, did not want to face Cash's anger. The argument had been terrible and personal and she was an interloper who had no right to have been a witness, but she was angry, too.

Swallowing her emotions, she turned to confront the man she'd come to love. His expression broke her heart, her anger dissolving in the face of his pain. His normally tan skin held a gray pallor. His full lips—which were quirked into a sardonic smile more often than not—drooped at the corners. His eyes were empty, bleak. His pain was almost visceral.

Her eyes filled with tears as she faced the despondent man—a man determined to hide his feelings, as desolate and lonely as that action might make him. Roxie wanted to run to him, wrap her arms around him, hold him. Tell him how she felt. She did none of those things. Anything of the sort would be rebuffed. She could tell by looking at his stiff posture.

"I'm sorry." She all but swallowed the last word trying to get it out around the lump in her throat.

"For what? For sneaking into my office?" Life came back into his eyes and they sparked with temper. "For watching me get eviscerated by my father? Mocked by my brothers?"

Anger, no matter how bitter or directed at her, was better than the defeat of a devastated man who looked like he'd been abandoned by his last friend. She stepped around the desk, wanting to be closer to him.

"I didn't sneak into your office. *You* asked me to meet you here and your assistant showed me in."

"Why the hell did you hide?" He stalked toward her but stopped after a couple of steps. His fists clenched at his sides and he was all but swaying with the effort to regain control.

"Uh, duh? You were with your father."

Cash frowned. "So?"

"After my last little run-in with the man, I figured it was better for us if he didn't find me in your office."

He scrubbed at his forehead with the heel of his palm and Roxie could almost see the headache forming. She wanted to make him sit down so she could rub his temples, massage his shoulders, kiss him. Something. Anything. Whatever it would take to make him understand he wasn't the worthless son his father accused him of being.

Cash, with studied casualness, skirted her location as he moved behind his desk and sank into the chair. "Sit down, Roxie," he said without looking at her.

She obeyed, sinking onto the edge of the nearest visitor's chair as Cash swiveled so that his back was partially to her and he could look out the window. Oklahoma City was spread out below—a blend of old and new, greenery and concrete, a place the Barrons considered their domain.

Silence stretched between them. She would have given anything to know what Cash was thinking. He was worlds away from the man he'd been the night before. The sex was always good, but last night had been special. He'd been tender. Loving. He'd shared his feelings with her. Today, that man no longer existed and her gut twisted up in greasy knots as she feared the worst.

"You shouldn't have hidden, Roxanne." Cash's voice was toneless.

"So, I should have stood here and defended our relationship?" Her chest was tight and her nose burned with tears threatening to appear. She knew what was coming, braced herself for his words.

"We don't have a relationship."

Cement solidified in her lungs, and she went cold as all her emotions drained away.

"I'll have Bridger arrange for someone to accompany you to the condo to pick up your things, take you and Harley home."

Roxie sat there too staggered by his proclamation to move. "You can't be serious. You're going to break us just like—" she snapped her fingers "—that? Are you joking?"

Now he turned to stare at her. His eyes held nothing but disdain. "I never joke, Roxanne. It was fun while it lasted but there was never any *us* to break. At this point in time, I don't need your assistance any longer, nor do I want you in my bed."

She was all but sputtering now. "My assistance? My *assistance*?" Her voice climbed in pitch and volume. "Is that what last night was? What the last few weeks spent in your bed, on the floor, in the shower, were?" Damn her red hair—for her temper and the way her skin colored when she was angry.

"I am not a prostitute, Cash. And you just made me feel like one. Maybe your father was right after all, because from where I'm standing? The apple didn't fall far from that tree."

She ducked around the desk, grasped the back of his chair and spun him around. Leaning down, she pinned him in by placing her hands on the arms of the chair. Spitting mad, she swallowed and narrowed her gaze on his eyes.

"You, Cashion Matthew Barron, are a major jerk. And you want to know something else? I think you try to be a major jerk. Look at your brothers. Clay is the leader. Cord is the responsible one. Chance is the smart one. Chase is the lovable rascal. And you? What is left for you? Being the jerk. In fact, I think you cultivate this whole persona because deep down, you're just a scared kid who—"

Cash grabbed her arms and shoved her backward as he surged up. Less than a second later, her back was pressed forcibly against the window glass and she was on her tiptoes. A mishmash of emotions suffused his face—anger, shock and, when his eyes dropped to her mouth, lust.

"Leave my brothers out of this."

"No. They are as much a part of this as your father is."

"You don't know anything about my family. About them. About him." He was growling the words and when he stopped to breathe, his chest pressed against hers. His whole body was vibrating from his barely-leashed anger. "And you know nothing about me. Nothing at all, Roxanne Rosetta Rowland."

Now his entire torso was pressed against her, chest to hips, and she was shocked to discover that Cash was aroused. A weird, detached part of her brain wondered if that was the reason angry make-up sex was so good.

"Let me go, Cash."

"No."

His grip on her biceps tightened and he lifted her high enough that her feet no longer touched the floor. Cash was scaring her a little but, positive she'd both touched a nerve and hit on the truth, Roxie pushed her luck. Cupping his face in her palms, she softened her voice.

"I know more than you think, Cash." She closed her eyes, let her own pain, her own fears, well up so they'd show. Then she raised her eyelids. "I know what having a bullying father is like, what it's like to have brothers who think you're nothing but a means to an end."

Cash loosened his fingers and her feet hit the floor. She dropped her hands when they started to tremble. Her voice was thick with suppressed hurt as she continued.

"You at least had your brothers, Cash, when you were growing up. You had Miz Beth and Big John after your mom died." He squeezed her arms again and his look turned fierce, but she wouldn't be deterred. This was too important. *He* was too important, and if they were ever to have a chance, she had to convince him of this.

"You had people who cared. I didn't. I never knew my mother. My father was a stranger and my brothers treated me like a stray puppy." She swallowed the spit that pooled in her mouth as she considered what she would reveal next.

"When I was five, my brother Dexter accused me of murdering our mother, of depriving the rest of them of her love. She died when I was born, you see." Roxie dropped her gaze, watched cars crawling along the street thirty-four floors below. "The next day, Lex—who was barely eighteen, by the way—loaded me into a car with one little plastic suitcase and drove me to a boarding school. He left me standing alone at the gate. I clutched my suitcase and watched the taillights disappear."

She dashed tears from her eyes, tears that blurred her sight when she really needed to be able to see Cash, to see his reaction. "You aren't the only orphan in this room, Cash. You aren't the only one who worries you aren't good enough to be loved."

"You're full of crap." He let go with one hand and ran it through his hair. His gaze moved from her to the vista outside the window. "I don't believe a word of this. You're as big a con as the rest of your family. Lies come out of your mouth as easily as you breathe."

Her heart was shredded into tiny pieces but at least her tears dried up from the force of the anger that overrode her anguish. "You don't get it, dumbass. Your father is a piece of work—as bad as mine, only yours claims to be legitimate in his feelings for you. That man wouldn't know love if Harley was covered in it and bit him on the butt. He's egotistical, hard, uncaring and a right royal bastard. Just like my father. Max Rowland lives for the game. The con—long or short. Using people and discarding them is his stock in trade. And I'm just one more asset to be used up and discarded. He has you in his sights and you know what? Despite everything you've said to me, I'll still do my best to protect the Barrons." She brushed her sleeve under her nose to avoid sniffling.

"I made a promise to you. To help you stop him. To stop my family, even if it means sending them to prison. And I will, regardless of what you think of me, or what you believe my motives to be."

Roxie jerked her other arm free and ducked away from Cash. "But there is a difference between your family and mine. A huge difference. My brothers only want to use me. But *your* brothers? They love you. A whole lot by everything I've seen. Mine are as bad as my father. They'll use me up and abandon me just like they did when I was five. Just like they did when I was sixteen. Just like they did in Vegas. You have a chance, Cash. A chance to be part of a family. A chance to be loved. Go make up with them while you can."

Cash's expression didn't change. She marched to the door, pulled it open and paused. "I'll get out of your life, but dude? Throwing me out is one of the biggest mistakes you'll ever make. In case you ever wake up and realize what an idiot you are, you know where to find me. Maybe you'll get lucky and I'll still love you. But you'd better be ready to crawl back. Groveling always works best."

She walked out, closed the door gently despite wanting to slam it. The darn thing was hung wrong for a dramatic exit. Placing her hand against the door in a final farewell, she called softly, "You can do it, Cash. You *can* find your family again."

Seventeen

Cash didn't remember covering the distance to the door. He leaned his forehead against it and heard Roxie's murmur. "How am I supposed to do that?" he asked the closed door.

Straightening, he wandered to the window and stared out. Taking a moment, he sent a text to Bridger. Any of the men hanging around the office could deal with Roxie, with getting her out of his life, but he didn't trust just any of them to do it right. He didn't hate her. No, he reserved that emotion for himself. Loathing what he'd become, he'd done what was needed. He knew all too well what his father's ultimatums meant.

Orders given, he remained at the window, ignoring both his phone and the pings coming from his computer whenever an email hit. He was done with the world for today, so he watched shadows grow, the spiked silhouette of the Barron Tower acting as a sundial. Roxie would be packed by now, her clutter cleared out of his condo. He wondered if Bridger had assigned Alan to her, then shoved those thoughts away.

He was a busy man. He didn't have time to moon over what might have been. Roxanne was the enemy; the Rowlands were out to harm the Barrons. She had to be in on it. Forget the sweet noises she uttered as he made love to her. Forget the way she made him laugh. Forget—

Cash banged his fist against the window hard enough to bruise the side of his hand. She was wrong! He couldn't fix things with his brothers. He was his father's son, through and through. His gut churned when he thought of the things he'd done in the name of family. Despicable. That's how Chance's wife, Cassidy, had described him, and she'd told the truth. He'd done everything his father asked of him. Everything. It didn't matter that he hurt the women his brothers loved. He hadn't cared that he'd betrayed the four men who deserved his absolute loyalty.

Family is the only thing that matters. How often had he heard his father spout those words? More importantly, when had he swerved from that premise to blindly follow his father's orders? He'd stopped questioning and just accepted that the old man was doing what was right for the family—for everyone *in* the family.

He paused his pity party long enough to text Bridger. He didn't get a reply.

A few lights flickered on below him. The Barrons pretty much owned everything within sight. But historically, what they had in business prowess, they lacked in their personal lives. At least that was the case for him and his father. Roxanne was wrong. His brothers didn't love him. They couldn't. Not after what he'd done. Because no matter what, Cash was his father's son. Cyrus had shaped him. Trained him. Molded him into the son he thought he wanted, only to discover Cash was a flawed creation.

By the time he left the office, hard dark had fallen and city lights painted an urban glow against the night sky. Cash should drink himself into a stupor. Yet going to a bar, even a quiet pub like Donovan's, didn't appeal and the thought of a nightclub filled with noise and crowds curdled his stomach. He should have just gone to his place but the thought of facing the empty space troubled him. He headed toward the ranch instead. He needed something—anything—that felt like home, and his vacant condo wasn't that. It would be filled with the lonely echoes of Roxie's presence, filled with what-ifs and what-might-have-beens.

Who was she to lecture Cash on the meaning of love? Or family? Her brutally honest recitation outlining her own childhood meant she had no more insight—and probably less—than he did. The families of her fellow boarding school "inmates" hadn't inspired confidence in families and love, either. But through it all, she'd remained a cockeyed optimist when it came to love. Love existed. Families supported one another, took care of one another.

Roxie caught glimpses of it from time to time, and since being in Cash's sphere of influence, she'd gotten firsthand experience. Miz Beth and Big John had been married fifty years and they were still as much in love as they were the day they pronounced their vows. Cash's brothers tended to avoid him, as did their wives. She hadn't forgotten the confrontation with three of them that time in Bricktown. While the women appeared angry, she still had the sense they were sad about the estrangement—that their husbands missed their brother. The Barron brothers seemed close-knit, at least the other four. Did Cash purposely hold himself apart from them or had they segregated him, like her brothers had her? She knew all about being the odd one out. She'd watched her brothers from afar, had seen how they all seemed so bonded, a pack of puppies tumbling around the feet of their father. And there was never time for her—no place for her in their testosterone-laced circle. She definitely had no right to spout off about family dynamics.

As she packed her things, to the accompaniment of Harley's soft grumbles, she tried not to think. Yeah, like that would ever work. Maybe this was a good thing, Cash sending her away. Her heart was growing way too fond of him, her dreams far too focused on a future with him. But there would be no future now. Or ever. Her fleeting hope of forming a family with him, of finding the kind of love she saw shared by his brothers and their wives, was just a pipe dream.

People like her weren't made for relationships. Evidently, neither were people like Cash. Harley, on the other hand, didn't want to leave. She understood his reluctance. She didn't want to go, either. Still, it was time. She couldn't stall any longer.

Roxie sat stiffly in the front seat of the Ford Expedition. The man who'd taken her to Cash's condo loaded the vehicle with her things and Harley, then drove with a reckless abandon that had her clenching her jaw more than once. And she didn't miss the side glances he angled in her direction. He'd rolled down a back window and now the Newf had his head stuck out, jowls and ears flopping in the wind.

Tired of the strained silence, she shifted in her seat to face Bridger Tate. She hadn't known him long and the taciturn man flummoxed her. She had no clue what he thought of her, of the way things had shaken out between her and Cash.

"Get it off your chest."

Bridger braked the SUV and idled at a stoplight. "Got nothing to say."

"Really?" She gave him the stink-eye. "Could have fooled me."

"He's my cousin, Roxanne. Family. What am I supposed to say?"

She flung out her hands. "I don't know. *You* must like him…" She studied his expression. "Or is it just because he's your boss?"

He glared at her so long the car behind them honked. The light had changed. He tromped the gas pedal and the big SUV jerked forward. "Yes, Cash is my boss. He's my cousin. He's also my friend."

"Huh." She packed a lot of sarcasm in that one syllable.

"What's that supposed to mean?"

"Seems like you and me are the only two around who actually like him."

"I'm not discussing this with you."

"Ah. Gotcha. I'm the outsider. The one he kicked out of his bed when his father snapped his fingers."

"That's not true."

"Were you there?"

Bridger stopped for another red light. Anger sculpted the planes of his handsome face. "No."

"Well, I was."

His head whipped around so fast she was worried he'd pull a muscle or something. "What do you mean? Uncle Cyrus threw his tantrum in front of you?"

She could actually feel the blush crawl up the skin of her throat and face. "Not exactly."

"Explain. Exactly." He sounded like a cop—or a drill sergeant.

"I was waiting for Cash in his office and I was sort of…um…looking at some stuff—"

"What stuff?" Bridger's eyes turned the color of a natural gas flame burning blue hot.

Roxie would have backpedaled if they'd been standing in a room. As it was, all she could do was press harder against the door to eke out extra space between them. Then she figured out why he was upset. "Oh! No, not *that* kind of stuff. No…no. I wouldn't… I wasn't spying. He has this really cool snow glo—"

"His mother gave that to him. He and Chase both had one. Chase broke his. It's the only thing Cash has left that belonged to Aunt Helen."

She pressed her lips between her teeth to help rein in her emotions. "That was his mother's name?"

Bridger nodded. "Yeah. Did he tell you how she died?" After she shook her head, he continued. "Drunk driver. She was DRT."

"DRT?"

"Dead right there. And it's weird, but I think Uncle Cyrus really was torn up by her death. At least according to my mom. He was still an SOB about things, but Mom says he mourned her."

"Huh. I think I might be surprised."

"I know, right?" Bridger winked as he divided his attention between her and traffic. "So…the snow globe?"

"Oh! Right. It's an intriguing piece, maybe even historically significant. I'd have to do some research to be sure—"

"Roxanne, I don't care. Get on with the story." She could hear the exasperation in his tone.

"Oh, right. So, I'm being nosy about the globe and I heard voices in the hall. I hadn't closed the door all the way when I got there because…well, you know the reason. I'm aware that none of you trust me. But the globe was so interesting and—"

"The voices, Roxanne." Bridger jerked her back on topic.

"Voices. Yes, outside. I…panicked. And hid. Under

Cash's desk. By the time I realized I should not be there, and did not want to hear what Cash and Mr. Barron were saying, it was too late. Announcing my presence would be far more awkward than just staying under the desk. I thought—hoped that Cash would leave with his father and I could sneak out, pretend I'd never been there and didn't hear a thing."

"But."

"*Huge* but. I suspect Cash knew I was there but I can't figure out how."

"Not that my cousin is OCD or anything but he knows with one glance whether someone has been in his office. You moved the globe."

"I did. In fact, I took it under the desk with me. Oh dear! Do you think Cash thought I was stealing it or something? I wasn't. Truly. And I put it right back in its spot on his desk when I stood up."

"No, Roxanne. I don't believe Cash thought you were trying to steal his snow globe."

"So he just…hates me now." Her insides were curled up like a ball of rattlesnakes and she didn't want to move, knowing she'd get all sorts of bites that would really hurt.

"I wish I could say you're wrong, Roxie, but I just don't know." He parked the SUV in front of her apartment and looked at her, his expression surprisingly sad. "I thought Cash might have a chance with you."

"A chance? I gave him all the chances in the world."

"That's not what I meant, hon. I meant that if my cousin smartened up, he'd take what you were offering. He needs what you could give him. I'm sorry he turned out to be an idiot."

He exited the vehicle on those words and silently unloaded her things, stacking them up on the small patio area next to her front door. Harley happily darted back and forth, following Bridger, then diverting to sniff the bushes.

Bridger set the sack of dog food down on the step and retreated without saying anything. He got in the driver's seat, started the SUV and backed out. Before pulling away, he stopped and rolled down his window. "You might have brought him back, Roxanne Rowland. It's a damn shame because you're right. I'm about the only one in the family who understands him—understands why he does what he does. And that makes me the only one who will stand for him when shit hits the fan. Take care of yourself."

Stunned, Roxie worked her mouth but no words came out. By the time they did, he was long gone.

"That was not the same man you left home with, sugar britches." The voice of her neighbor floated down from on high. "How many times have I told you that you come home with the one that brought you?"

"Hi, Leo." She sounded as deflated as she probably looked as she stepped closer to the parking lot so she could see him.

Leo eyed her pile of belongings from his perch on his balcony. "Oh, honeybun." He sighed. "Please don't tell me that you blew your chance with that grade A prime piece of man."

"Okay. I won't."

"Girl, I thought I taught you better. How did you manage to screw things up?"

"I wish I knew."

Eighteen

Roxanne stared into her coffee cup. How could she have been so totally wrong about Cash?

"You're giving up on him." The chiding tone of Miz Beth's voice whipped across her nerves like an electric wire. The woman had shown up on her doorstep and Roxie hadn't known how to politely send her away.

"Do I have a choice?"

With her eyes closed, Roxie bent her head back in a vain attempt to ease her cramped neck muscles. "He threw me out, Miz Beth, and frankly? The things I've heard about what he did to his sisters-in-law?"

"I thought better of you, Roxanne."

She tossed her hands up to emphasize her exaggerated shrug. "Why am I the bad guy here?"

"Do you love him?" Miz Beth was relentless.

"I don't know. I thought I did, but after what he said about me, about us? I thought I knew him, Miz Beth, but I don't know him at all."

"Neither do his brothers, or their wives." The woman sniffed, her displeasure apparent.

Roxanne was dismayed. "How can you defend him?"

"Because I see what everyone else ignores." Miz Beth settled into her chair. "I see the lonely boy who only wants to be loved."

"He has a funny way of looking for love."

"His brothers believe he is without remorse. Their wives think that not only are his actions despicable, but that he actually enjoyed hurting them." Miz Beth's gaze softened. "That boy feels far more and far deeper than the lot of 'em."

Confused, Roxanne worked through the meanings behind the older woman's words—the woman who was his surrogate mother, the one who'd told Roxie not long ago that she loved every one of "her" boys. Everything she'd learned about Cash's brothers pointed to the fact that they loved their wives, loved one another. Deeply. All four couples shared an abiding loyalty, with Cash standing on the outside. Like she and her family.

"Right or wrong, Cash does what he does out of a sense of duty. He decided at some point that he has to protect them all. Sometimes from themselves, but more often than not from their father."

"Would Mr. Barron do something terrible to them?" Cyrus Barron was a force to be reckoned with but Roxie didn't believe he'd actually carry out his threats on his own blood.

Miz Beth sipped her coffee, and sadness settled around her like a shawl made of shadows. She ignored Roxie's questions. "Those terrible things Cash has done? Would you like to know why he did them?"

Roxanne nodded, her throat closing in reaction to the expression on Miz Beth's face.

"Because Cyrus Barron decreed they had to be done, and Cash took the tasks upon himself to save his brothers from having to do them."

"I...don't understand."

"Everything Cash did, it was at Cyrus's orders—orders he'd given to the other boys first. Cash stepped in and did the things his brothers couldn't stomach, and he didn't do it because he's a bad man. He did it to shield his brothers from their father's wrath. In fact, that boy has taken the brunt of it—from Cyrus and every last one of his brothers."

"Why would his father...? I'm not following, Miz Beth."

"Cyrus wants to control his sons. When Chance first defied him, that vile old man would have destroyed him. But Cash stepped in."

"So Chance didn't have to—and..." Roxie's brain whirled through the possibilities. "Chance would have destroyed any possibility of a relationship with Cassie."

"Precisely. I knew you were a smart one." The woman pushed away from the table, stood and went to retrieve the coffee pot. Miz Beth refilled her cup, offering one to Roxanne, who shook her head. She wasn't sure she could swallow around the lump in her throat.

Miz Beth sighed. "They were all so angry at him."

Her soft *humph* was both sad and telling. "No one ever accused the Barrons of having easy tempers. Ever last one of 'em goes off like a firecracker. Cash wants his father to love him. He's never figured out that it's a lost cause like the other boys have. They got smart, decided it didn't matter. But when Cyrus decided to stop his sons from falling in love, Cash stepped up to shield his brothers. Every time. Cash is the one who feels the duty to be a good son the most—no matter what terrible things Cyrus orders him to do."

"They've all but cut him out of their lives because of that, haven't they?" That knot clogging Roxanne's throat grew bigger.

Miz Beth's eyes glistened with tears. "They may not mean to, but they do. Every day. In little ways. Ways they don't realize, but he does. He feels their rejection. Those boys just… They broke his heart. He stood there in my kitchen, hiding from the rest of the family the night his own twin renewed his marriage vows in front of the whole family. Cash hadn't been invited, had been told by Cord and Chance to stay away, given what he'd done in an attempt to break up Chase and Savannah."

Roxie had to blink her own tears away. "That's…" She inhaled and exhaled in an attempt to ease the constriction in her chest. "I don't know what it is."

"It's sad and cruel. But he came, slipping in at the last minute. He stood in the shadows and listened and wished his brother well. And just as fast, he disappeared again. We had a big Christmas at the ranch but Cash wasn't present. He wasn't welcome in his own home. Then or now. I've seen him turn around and leave when he comes up the drive and sees one of the others is there."

"That's...that's just mean and...and..."

"Don't get me wrong, Roxanne. Cash isn't an angel. Heck, none of those boys are. Cash, though? He listens to his father way too much, and while his actions are bad, his heart truly is in the right place—as he understands things. Trying to take Cassie's inheritance. That whole custody kidnapping of CJ. Setting up Clay and then Chase so Georgie and Savannah thought their men were cheating on them. It wasn't right. I think Cash knew that but his concept of right and wrong is skewed thanks to the old jackass who sired him." Miz Beth dumped her coffee in the sink. "You have a lot of thinking to do, girl. And it's a long drive back to the ranch."

The woman was right. Roxie did have a lot to consider. "Thanks for coming by, Miz Beth."

"Any time, sugar. Any time at all."

They'd reached the door when Miz Beth spoke again. "Roxanne, if ever a man needs to be loved—deserves to be loved, it's Cashion Barron."

Those parting words played over and over in her mind. Cash deserved to be loved, and she did. She didn't know exactly when, and sure couldn't figure out how, given his prickly personality, but she loved him with all her heart.

Nineteen

Cash braked for the stoplight, angry that he couldn't even enjoy lunch at Donovan's without memories of Roxie intruding. His phone pinged and he checked the caller ID, then answered. "Hey, Bridger, did you get—"

"Cash." The dire tone of Bridger's voice saying only his name had him maneuvering into the parking lot of a fast-food restaurant. He stopped haphazardly and shoved the Rover into Park.

"What's going on, Bridge?"

"It's…your father. I found him. In the parking garage. It's bad, Cash. I couldn't call before now. I was doing CPR."

CPR? Cash went cold but his skin prickled from nerves and dread. He couldn't speak and Bridger filled in the silence.

"Fire department got here fast. The ambulance just left. They're taking him to the ER at OU Med Center. It… I'm sorry, Cash. They're still doing CPR. The defibrillator didn't get a blip when they zapped his heart. You need to meet me there. Okay?"

"Okay." The word came out flat, robotic. Cash couldn't feel a thing.

"I'll call your brothers."

Something sparked in his brain, shoving aside his shock. "No. I should call. I'll… I'm on Western. I'll be there in twenty minutes. Less."

"I can send someone to pick you up." Concern coated his cousin's voice.

"No. I'm okay. I… I need to call Chase. The others. I'll see you at the hospital." He ended the call to Bridger, then scrolled through his contacts. He started at the top.

Clay's phone rolled over to voice mail. Cash managed to keep his voice level. "Clay, it's about Dad. He's at OU Med. I don't know what happened. Bridger did CPR before they transported him. Probably his heart. I…thought you should know. Thought you might want to come."

He called Cord, got voice mail and left the same message. Ditto with Chance, but with each successive call, it was harder to keep his voice steady. Under normal circumstances, he would have called their administrative assistants, knowing they'd delegated contact with him to their employees. But this was far from normal and he couldn't—wouldn't—do that to his brothers. They might not want to talk to him, obviously didn't want anything to do with him, but he would not tell them their father was most likely dying through the filter of an employee.

Breathing became hard, his chest tight and aching. He didn't love his father—not in the sense most sons did, but the man had sired him, raised him, taught him hard lessons. All he'd ever wanted was to have his father's respect, his acceptance. Cash knew, deep down, that Cyrus Barron was incapable of loving anyone but himself, but Cash had always held out hope that someday, he'd do something to make his father proud.

Cash had one more call to make. He punched the link for his twin. This time he got a live person, but not the one he wanted.

"Cash. What's up?"

"I need to talk to Chase, Tucker. Please?" The last word came out as a plea.

"He's…busy. I can pass him your message."

Busy. His twin brother wouldn't even talk to him. Cash closed his eyes, rubbed them with his fingers, ignoring the moisture dampening his fingertips. He'd never felt so isolated and alone in his life.

"Cash? Is there a message?"

"Tell him…tell him I…" He swallowed so many words that wouldn't come out. What could he say? *I'm sorry? Dad's dying? I'm as big a bastard as our old man and maybe I should be the one the doctors are working on? I love you?* He heard his cousin breathing. No help there. "Tell him Dad is at OU Med. I'm headed to the ER. It's…not good. Bridger had to do CPR. I…thought everyone would want to know."

Silence. Yeah. No one in his family would give a

rat's ass that his father was in the ER, fighting for his life. His cousin's lack of response was far more telling than any comment. "Sorry I bothered y'all, Tucker."

He ended the call, inhaled and held his breath until his hands stopped shaking enough that he could drive. Twenty-two minutes later, he walked into the ER. Bridger stood off to the side of the waiting room. For the biggest ER in the metro area, the place was almost eerily quiet. His cousin's face pretty much said it all.

"The doctors are working on him," Bridger said as Cash walked up. "I have a security team coming. It's just a matter of time before the media get wind of this."

Yeah. The media. Vultures of every stripe would be circling soon. "Your mom?"

"I called her. She's in Belize but headed home now." Bridger waited a moment before adding, "Your brothers?"

Seemingly of its own volition, Cash's head bowed. He rubbed the back of his neck and mumbled, "I left voice mails. No one was answering. I did talk to Tucker. Chase—" His voice broke. "Chase was too busy."

Embarrassed by his lapse in control, Cash walked away. He had too much pent-up energy to sit, but pacing just drew unwanted attention. He dropped into a chair in the far corner of the ER waiting room and hunched over, his elbows resting on his thighs, head bowed. Wrapping his misery around him as if it would make him invisible, Cash stared at the floor and tried not to think.

Roxie stopped in the break room to refill her travel mug with coffee. Four coworkers stood staring at the

TV mounted to the wall and she stopped to listen to the breaking news.

"Oklahoma City billionaire Cyrus Barron was rushed to OU Medical Center ER this afternoon in unknown condition. Witnesses stated that a member of Mr. Barron's security team found the businessman unconscious in the parking garage of Barron Tower and began CPR. A hospital spokeswoman will only confirm that Mr. Barron was admitted to the ER." The perky blonde went on with her recitation but Roxie had tuned everything out.

Mr. Barron was in the ER? They'd done CPR? Cash. He'd be there all alone. She didn't stop to think. Dumping her cup in the sink, Roxie whirled and headed for the exit. More people had gathered to watch the report, blocking her way, and the VP she reported to was already in crisis mode.

"We'll need to put a package together—photos and video of his life for media release. Contact Chase Barron or Tucker Tate. They'll have the obit and other information." He pointed at Roxie. "Good. You're here. You can pull up the file documents faster than the rest of us—"

"No." Roxie had no idea where the strength to stand up to her boss came from but she was fairly vibrating with it. "I can't. Get one of my assistants to do it. I have to go."

"Go?" The man looked flummoxed.

"Cash. I have to get to the hospital." He might not want to see her, would probably try to throw her out, but she was not going to let him sit there all alone waiting for word on his father. "I…sorry. I have to go," she repeated.

"They're dating," she heard someone explain as she ducked through the door and jogged toward the elevator. That wasn't true. They'd never…*dated.* But when she'd been moved into his condo and he'd informed her bosses he needed her for a "special" project, they'd leaped to an obvious conclusion. They'd be horrified to discover that Cash had only wanted information about her family. Well, that and sex. What he hadn't wanted was her falling in love with him. Too bad. For both of them.

Roxie stopped in her office long enough to grab her purse and keys, then made the dash to the medical center complex on Lincoln Boulevard. She gave up on the ER parking lot, driving around to the garage complex on the back side of the hospital. All four local television stations had live remotes going outside the ER doors and two uniformed policemen stood just outside monitoring anyone going in or out. Knowing what she'd learned about Barron Security, Cash would have a team inside the ER to protect his family.

She waited, watching people come and go for a few minutes. The police didn't stop anyone unless they looked like media. She was fully prepared to lie her way inside, up to and including faking an injury or illness. Turned out, all she had to do was keep her head down and look puzzled at the reporters all doing live feeds. The officers gave her cursory glances, she dipped her head in acknowledgment of their presence and scurried through the automatic doors.

Bridger Tate stood across the room speaking into his

phone, his eyes darting between the door and a spot in the far corner. A man in a dark suit stood a few feet away from him. Roxie wondered for a minute if Senator Barron got Secret Service protection. Bridger eyed her speculatively and she offered a tentative smile even as she picked out two more men and a woman, all in various types of civilian clothes and spread throughout the room.

Her gaze came to a rest on Cash and she forced air into her lungs. He looked so lost and forlorn. She was already walking toward him before her brain caught up with her instincts. The woman came to her feet and moved to intercept, but a sign from Bridger waved the female security guard off. Roxie sank onto the chair next to Cash. She didn't speak, didn't touch him though she was desperate to do both.

"Go away, Roxie." Cash didn't look at her and his voice sounded like a rusty nail being yanked out of wood.

"You shouldn't be alone."

He glanced up and his upper lip curled into a snarl. "Does it look like I'm alone?"

"Except for Bridger? Yes."

"Goes to show what you know."

And as if in answer to his rebuttal, the entrance doors whispered open. Two angry Barron brothers ate up the distance and stopped in front of them.

"What the hell, Cash?" Cord demanded.

Roxie was about to choose discretion over valor when Cash stood and brushed his older brother back. "Dad had a heart attack. They're working on him."

Before Cord could respond, Cash pushed past him and moved to the opposite corner. The two elder Barrons exchanged looks but didn't follow him. They ignored Roxie, walking instead to Bridger, where they spoke in low tones she couldn't overhear. She was still sitting there hunched in on herself when the ER doors opened and the doctor stepped through. The Barrons gathered around him.

Roxie watched Cash crumple, then straighten. He shook off his brothers and stormed out into the night. Wearily, she pushed out of her chair and headed after him. Bridger stopped her halfway to the door.

"Let him be, Roxie. For now at least. I know Cash. He'll want to be alone."

She turned her tear-streaked face to the one other person in the room who cared about Cash. "But isn't that the problem? He's always alone."

Roxie slipped into the funeral home hoping for the chance to see Cash before the service started. Wandering down a hallway, she heard voices coming her direction. Finding an alcove with a drawn curtain, she ducked behind it, planning to wait until the people moved on. When the group stopped right in front of her hiding place and she recognized the voices, she cringed.

"I did not appreciate finding out my father was in the hospital after suffering a massive heart attack when my wife called to tell me it was the lead story on all the news channels. Georgie had us packed by the time I got home from the Senate building."

"I caught a report on the radio coming back from a

rig. Jolie wasn't on duty at the hospital so she had no idea."

"I was in court. One of the court clerks brought a note to the judge and he called an in-camera hearing at the bench. The damn judge knew before I did."

Clay, Cord and Chance, in that order. She'd seen Cord and Chance at the hospital, knew they'd gotten word fairly quickly to get there when they did. Far too curious for her own good, Roxie peeked around the edge of the curtain.

The three stared at Chase, who appeared thoughtful. "Did any of you check your missed calls or your voice mails?" The older brothers exchanged looks. "I'll admit I haven't wanted to deal with Cash, and that includes talking to him even with all this BS going on with the Rowlands. I had his calls forwarded to Tucker's cell." A look of sadness settled on Chase's face—a face so like Cash's Roxie's heart broke all over again. "Tuck answered. Cash...he was broken up. Hurting. Tuck didn't know what to do so he didn't do anything. Didn't say anything. When Cash ended the call, Tuck called me immediately." He rubbed the back of his neck, a gesture so achingly familiar Roxie almost cried.

Clay, Cord and Chance went for their phones and started scrolling. Then they each listened to the message left by Cash. At least they looked remorseful now.

"What are we going to do?" Cord glanced around the circle, but rested his final gaze on Chase.

"We do what this family has always done," Clay said. "We present a united front. Then, when we're in private, we'll figure it out."

Their wives arrived and Roxie faded deeper into the alcove. They walked away, en masse, presenting their united front. Only Cash wasn't with them. A Garth Brooks song played in her head, the words so fitting. Yeah, Cash was standing outside the fire. And he was facing his world all alone.

A few minutes later, after no sign of Cash, she settled in the last row of pews in the chapel. The family entered from the right and filled the first several rows, the four Barron brothers and wives in the first pew with Miz Beth and Big John. The next few rows were filled with cousins and Mr. Barron's sister. Still no sign of Cash. Then Roxie caught movement on the opposite side. Cash entered from the left and sat down in the empty front pew, as far away from his family as he could sit.

Roxie grabbed the box of tissues sitting on the seat next to her and pulled out a handful as tears spilled over. She'd never seen anyone look more dejected—and *rejected* than Cash Barron at that moment. The service and eulogies went on interminably. She heard the disparaging whispers about Cash from those sitting around her.

When it was finally over, Cash slipped away once more. She waited in the reception hall, just in case, but Cash never appeared. Oh, but his brothers were all there, accepting condolences. They'd finally retreated to a spot away from the remaining crowd. When she saw Chase laugh at something Cord said, she lost her temper.

Roxie didn't stop to think, didn't consider her actions. She marched right up to the lot of them and snarled, "You know, for seemingly intelligent men, the four of you are pretty damn stupid."

The wives bristled, moving to stand with their husbands, and Cassidy scowled at her. "Now wait just a minute—"

In no mood for their resentment, Roxie cut her off. "You have no clue what Cash has done for you, each and every one of you. And what did you do? You turned your back on him. You never once asked him why he did the things he did. You just assumed he was the bad guy. You ostracized him." Her temper was riding her hard and her nose was running from unshed tears. She whirled on Chance. "Want to know why Cash served those legal papers? So you wouldn't have to, so your father would get off your back and you'd have a chance with Cassidy because you were the good guy."

Roxie pointed a finger at Cord and Jolie. "And you two? You should talk to your little boy. He has some mighty interesting ideas about his uncle Cash's motives. You know what they say, out of the mouths of babes.

"And no offense, Senator, but who do you think your staff called to arrange to get you back to Oklahoma so fast? It was Cash who made the arrangements. And it was Cash who installed a discreet guard at the hospital the whole time Georgie was a patient. To make sure she stayed safe."

Clay glowered at her, his mouth pinched. "How do you know all this?"

"That's not important. What *is* important is that you all wake up! Cash did all the dirty work your father wanted each of you to do. He *protected* you. He protected you so well that he walked away from me to keep that rotten old man happy. He loves you four so much he won't let himself be loved because somebody has to be the bad guy. And bad guys don't deserve to be loved. Not by anybody."

Blinking hard and breathing around the ache in her chest, she fixed her gaze on Chase. "You didn't even invite him to your wedding."

"Well, no one was invited—"

"Not the one in Vegas. The one at the ranch. Did you know—" she paused to glare at Cord and Chance "—that your brothers warned him to stay away. Insisted on it, in fact."

Chase paled while his brothers exchanged guilty looks. "But I saw him there, in the kitchen."

"Yeah, he sneaked in the back door. He stood there in the shadows of the kitchen watching you exchange vows with the woman you loved, because you're brothers. Because he's your twin and no matter what he's done or said, he freaking loves you. All of you. Not that you deserve it."

She sniffled and swiped at her cheeks. Tears fell freely now. "I thought my family was pretty messed up but you Barrons? I don't have an adjective vile enough for any of you."

Wheeling, she managed one step before a firm but gentle hand snagged her arm. "Ms. Rowland? Roxanne, please…a moment?"

Shaking with anger, she held still but refused to look at Cash's twin.

The hand on her arm remained, as if Chase needed a connection to her when he asked, "Do you love him?"

Her lips trembled and her chin quivered as she tried to form words. She finally managed a whispered, "Yes."

"Then go find him and tell him."

Twenty

After the funeral, Roxanne had no contact with any of the Barrons. Cash ignored her repeated attempts to contact him. Life settled into an unsettled routine. Harley missed Cash almost as much as she did. He slept on her bed and while he was almost as big and far warmer, he was a poor substitute. Almost a month had passed and she was in a meeting when the text came. She didn't reply for an hour, waiting until she was safely back in her office. Then she typed a one-word reply.

NO.

Her phone rang almost immediately and she answered with, "What part of no don't you understand, Dexter?"

"You want to keep your boyfriend safe, you'll use the tickets, Rox."

"He's not my boyfriend." She was proud her voice didn't waver, even though her heart was pounding. Cash was out of her life for good but the idea of him being hurt because of her? Unthinkable. She didn't doubt for a minute that Dexter would do something awful to Cash. Besides, she'd made a promise to keep the Barron family safe.

Putting all her acting abilities to use, she put steel in her voice. "I'm done with Cash, with all the Barrons, Dex. And I'm done with you."

"Yeah, but you care about the pretty boy so you'll come. Info's in your inbox." Her brother hung up.

Opening her email, she scanned the message, extrapolating what Dex actually meant from what was said. Then she picked up the desk phone and dialed.

"Where's Cash?" she asked when Bridger answered.

"Vegas."

"Of course he is." Her family knew that. They were putting the plot into action, and she had her own part to play. "It's time. I'll send you the details."

"Good."

Good for the Barrons. Not so good for her. She would fulfill her promise but then even the tenuous link she had with Cash would be gone. Time to say goodbye to the future she'd barely dreamed of before her hopes were crushed. Once a con, always a con. Isn't that what her family said? "It's in your blood, Rox. It's in your blood."

Cash occupied a seat at the small bar against the back wall of the Crown Hotel and Casino's main floor.

The scotch on the rocks in front of him had remained untouched so long the "rocks" had melted. He caught the stir near the entrance to the slot machine room and stiffened.

She walked in like she owned the place and every man in the room came to attention. Including him. Shifting his hips in his chair to give his rapidly growing erection a little breathing room, Cash watched the sea of bodies part as she sauntered toward him. Roxanne Rowland fixed him with a sultry stare. Gone was the klutzy girl. This was the woman only hinted at on the security footage he'd watched months ago. She wore red. And sparkles. The dress barely covered her, the floaty material swirling around legs made longer by red stilettos.

Part of his brain wondered, not for the first time, which Roxie was real. Had he made a mistake about her? He remembered something Roxie said the first time he questioned her in his office. "Takes a con to catch a con." The muttered reminder didn't make him feel any better.

He should have stood up, intercepted her, but Cash didn't move. He sat, alert and focused, watching her weave through the crowded room, her gaze holding his. *Eye on the prize*, he thought. She arrived in front of him, placed her hands on his knees and applied a little pressure to open a space for her to stand between them. Her hands slid up his thighs as she leaned in. Her lips grazed his cheek on their way to his ear.

"I've missed you," she murmured.

"Missed you, too."

Roxie gave no indication she heard him, so maybe he hadn't confessed that out loud. He could barely admit it to himself, much less expose his weakness to her.

"I'm supposed to seduce you and lure you to a room upstairs."

"I see."

She pressed closer and he widened his legs until their lower bodies touched. Her swift intake of breath was a sure sign she'd felt his arousal.

"You've been their target all along. I don't know why, but if you'll come with me, we'll find out."

Cash slipped an arm around her, anchoring her against him. "And I should just trust you?"

He felt the hitch of her breath as her body tensed. "No, I suppose you shouldn't. I'm a Rowland, right? But you can trust your family. Trust Bridger."

She brushed glossy red lips across his mouth. "I'm sorry." The words whispered across his skin. Her fingers twined with his resting on her hip, and she twirled away, tugging him to his feet.

Unable to resist, he followed her. Cash heard the murmurs as they passed. "Lucky SOB." He didn't feel lucky; he felt more like a lamb being led to slaughter. They entered an empty elevator and he recognized Bridger's hand in that. Once the doors closed, she dropped his hand, pushed a button and moved to the far corner, putting as much distance between them as possible.

"Smile for the camera, Cash, so they know I haven't drugged you or something."

He expected her to sound bitter—or sarcastic. She

sounded resigned. Glancing up at the camera, he pretended he didn't miss her warmth, the touch of her hand. As the elevator settled to a gentle stop, she returned, slipping under his arm and plastering herself against his side.

"They'll be watching," she said by way of explanation.

The back of his neck prickled as they exited. Cash didn't see anyone but he didn't doubt her. They strolled down the thickly carpeted hallway arm in arm. Stopping at the door to a suite, she produced a key card from the soft folds of fabric covering her breasts. Cash shifted uncomfortably. This wasn't about the sexy woman standing next to him. This was business.

The lock clicked and he pushed the door open all the way. She stretched to whisper in his ear. "We have to make it look good. Just go with it, okay?"

More curious than apprehensive now, he wondered if this was some elaborate ruse Roxie had cooked up to get close to him. He followed her into the living area. She turned and one crystal-encrusted strap dipped off her shoulder. She wet her lips and he almost groaned. She looked wanton and he wanted her more than anything he'd ever desired in his life.

"You got me up here, Roxanne. Now what?"

"Now we make a deal." Max Rowland stepped out of the bedroom.

Cash did his best to look surprised, then he raised a sardonic eyebrow. Someone knocked on the door and Max added, "Get that, Roxie girl. It'll be your brothers."

"What deal, Rowland?"

"You and my sentimental daughter cost me a great deal of time, money and annoyance six years ago. It's taken me this long to get plans in place."

"Ah. I see. You're still holding a grudge because I recovered everything you swindled from my great-aunt."

"I don't hold grudges, Barron. I get even."

Cash moved away as Roxanne returned, followed by her brothers and...his intern, Nick? What the hell?

Max wore a Cheshire-cat smile. "I see you recognize my youngest son, Nixon."

He glanced toward Roxie. Her face had drained of color and she looked devastated. There was no way she could fake the emotions warring on her face. She didn't know. And his own vetting process had failed. There'd been no record of any other Rowlands when they were trying to track down Max and his sons.

The college intern Cash knew as Nick England had fooled them all. The guy didn't look much like his brothers and looked nothing at all like Roxie. She'd locked her knees to remain standing but he could see the hands clasped in front of her tremble. He wanted to cross to her, hold her, but he couldn't. Not yet.

"So you wasted all these years just to put a mole in my organization? Why? Nick—Nixon didn't have access to anything confidential that would do you any good."

"Au contraire, Cashion," Max said in a perfect imitation of Cyrus's voice. "I'd say things are a little strained at the moment."

"What do you want?"

"Twenty million. Transferred to an offshore account."

Cash snorted in disgust. "And what do I get out of it?"

Nixon approached with a thick file. "You get to save your family one more time."

Accepting the file, Cash moved toward the built-in bar. He snagged Roxanne's hand as he passed and drew her along in his wake. Settling her on a bar stool, he put the file on the granite bar top and flipped through it. He should have given Nick more credit. The kid was good. He'd dummied up deals, laid a trail of under-the-table payments, double accounting books—all things the IRS and Justice Department would kill to get their hands on.

Cash raised his head to stare at Max. "Nice little web you've built here."

"Twenty million makes it all go away."

"For how long?"

The Cheshire cat once more, Max grinned. "Until we need more."

"And if I say no?"

"Copies will inconveniently show up several places—the government, rival media outlets. I wonder what the Senate ethics committee would make of this? Nevada gaming commission? EPA?" Max's eyes cut to Roxie. "And my daughter will be implicated as your coconspirator."

Her sharp intake of breath was almost silent but Cash heard it, and then felt her stiffen, then collapse next to him. Yeah, she was right. His father had been a cold and vicious piece of work but her father was ten times the monster.

"So you're saying Roxanne had nothing to do with this?"

Max and his sons all laughed, but it was Dexter who explained. "The stupid twit is too sentimental and honest. We set her up just like we did you. If she'd just hidden that stuff all those years ago, we'd all be in the clear."

Cash's frigid smile rivaled Max's. "That's all I needed to know."

Before anyone could move, hotel security and Las Vegas cops poured through the door. Within moments, the Rowlands were handcuffed and marched out. Cash stood frozen in place as he realized all of his brothers were there. It was Chase who approached.

"An apology is pretty meaningless, Cash, even when it comes from the heart. I'm sorry. For everything. I had no idea…" Chase gestured toward their other brothers. "*We* had no idea, but we should have. We knew what the old man was like, how he could twist things. And we left you hanging."

A moment later, Cash was swallowed in Chase's hug, then the rest of his brothers stepped up to offer their own apologies and hugs. Family. He'd found his again and he had to blink back tears. A flash of red caught his attention. Roxie. She slipped out the door without a word or a backward glance.

Chase chuckled and clapped him on the back. "Go after her, Cash. And when you're ready, I just happen to know a Liberace impersonator who does weddings."

Cash caught up to Roxanne at the elevator. "Where ya goin', Red?"

The door opened and he stepped in with her, keying

in the code for the top floor. She eyed him warily and he couldn't blame her. "I'm sorry." Apologies never came easy and he was surprised the words didn't stick in his throat. "I'm sorry your family betrayed you. I'm sorry I…" Now it got hard. "I should have trusted you. And I was wrong. I need you, Roxie. And I want you. What do I need to do to get you to forgive me?"

She silently got off the elevator with him when it stopped. He led her to his suite and ushered her inside. He smiled, remembering her parting words. "How much groveling will it take?"

That startled a laugh out of her, and he saw the insecurity, saw her own need for acceptance and love. She was everything he wanted and didn't know how to find. She had so many layers and he wanted to spend the rest of his life peeling them back, discovering the fascinating woman she was. She fit him in ways no one else ever had, or ever would.

Fingering the sparkly straps of her dress, he slipped them off her shoulders, pushed the silky dress down, found the clasp under the crystal-covered brooch at her hip and watched the dress float to the floor around her ankles. He cupped her cheeks, kissed her gently despite his overwhelming need to take her, conquer her, claim her. He needed to be gentle.

"I want to make love to you."

She nodded and slipped out of her heels, stepped over the puddled silk. He picked her up, carried her to the bed. She watched him strip out of his clothes, then he joined her. Cash drew her to him, stroking her hair back from her face. An unfamiliar emotion welled up.

Love. This must be what love felt like. He kissed her, cupped her, stroked and petted until she sighed, the long, contented sound of it a balm on his wounded heart.

He vowed to cherish her because no one ever had. It was easy to be tender, to put the dreamy look in her eyes he now enjoyed. He would spend his life proving how precious she was to him—if she'd give him the chance.

Using all his skill, he teased her until she was begging.

"Please, Cash. Inside me now. Please!"

"Not yet. Not until you say you'll marry me."

"Marry you?"

"Yes. Marry me."

"That's blackmail."

"A man's gotta do what a man's gotta do."

Roxie laughed, as if she couldn't help it. "Yes." She giggled, then her breath caught as he slid deep inside her. "Oh, yes," she moaned. "Just like that."

He rocked against her and caught a glint of mischief in her golden eyes. "What?"

"I should tell you something."

"Oh?" He pulled almost free of her.

"Yeah. The only reason I said yes is because Harley likes you."

"So…if that walking furbag didn't like me, you would have said no?" He held still, hovering, barely holding their connection.

"I would have agreed to a mad affair." He reached between them, found the spot guaranteed to drive her wild. "Maybe agreed to be your mist—aah." She sucked in her breath, quivering as she arched her hips against his touch.

"You love me. Admit it." The need in his voice surprised him, and from the look on Roxie's face, it caught her off guard, too.

She hooked her legs around him, her heels pushing against his butt until he was seated deeply inside her again. "With all my heart. I love you."

Cash gritted his teeth, struggling to hold back. Being with Roxie, connecting to her emotionally and physically…it hijacked his self-control. "I love you. And it's my duty to make you happy." He growled the words, pumping into her furiously now. He drove them both over the edge and when they fell back to earth, he discovered something precious.

"Home," he murmured. "You feel like home, Roxie."

Epilogue

Harley was on his best behavior, though he watched the swimming pool with obvious gusto. Cash stared until the dog eyed him guiltily and sat down next to the judge. Cash waited under a rustic arbor made of branches and twined with flowers, flanked by his solemn brothers. Well, all but Chase. Cash's twin grinned like a fool.

All the Tates were in attendance, some with plus-ones. His sisters-in-law sat together. More fences needed to be mended there. He'd promised Roxie he'd try, and she'd promised to help. His gaze fell on Kade Waite, and he recognized a kindred spirit. He resolved to look into that situation, too. The man who might be a Barron brother stood off to the side with Pippa Duncan. Interesting.

At that moment, Leo, looking like a fashion plate in his dove-gray tuxedo, emerged from the house. Big John appeared, Roxie on his arm. Deacon strummed a complicated melody on an acoustic guitar as Cash's bride glided toward him.

Their vows were simple. They promised to remain true to each other in good times and bad, in sickness and in health, through failures and triumphs. They vowed to respect, comfort and encourage, to dream, share and cherish, for as long as they lived. Then the judge pronounced them husband and wife. Cash branded Roxie with his kiss, one as deep and abiding as his love for this woman.

After dinner, Leo stood and pinged a champagne flute with his fork. "I need y'all's attention!" When he had it, he turned to Roxie. "Girlfriend, I am so happy you finally took my advice and snagged this fine, *fine* piece of man candy." He sniffled dramatically and dabbed at his eyes. "You make me so proud." He tossed back the champagne in his glass and sat.

Chase rose next, waiting while people quieted. "To my brother Cash and his beautiful bride. From this day forward, you will never walk alone. May your heart shelter the other always and may you always find your way home in each other's arms."

Lifting Roxie's left hand, Cash kissed her wedding ring. "You are my home, Roxanne Barron. You are my life, my heart, the very best of me. Now and always."

He brushed her tears away with his thumbs as he cupped her face and kissed her. They'd both searched all their lives for love and acceptance, and had found them in each other. She whispered against his lips, "You are my home and family. I love you."

Those were the words he needed. Together, they discovered the family they hadn't dared dream of. "Yes," he agreed. He was a man who understood his duty to family—and to the woman he loved.

* * * * *

*If you loved this story,
pick up the other* RED DIRT ROYALTY *books
from Silver James!*

*COWGIRLS DON'T CRY
THE COWGIRL'S LITTLE SECRET
THE BOSS AND HIS COWGIRL
CONVENIENT COWGIRL BRIDE*

Available now from Harlequin Desire!

***

*If you're on Twitter, tell us what you think
of Harlequin Desire! #harlequindesire.*

COMING NEXT MONTH FROM

HARLEQUIN

Desire

Available April 4, 2017

#2509 THE TEN-DAY BABY TAKEOVER
Billionaires and Babies • by Karen Booth
When Sarah Daltry barges into billionaire Aiden Langford's office with his secret baby, he strikes a deal—help him out for ten days as the nanny and he'll help with her new business. Love isn't part of the deal...

#2510 EXPECTING THE BILLIONAIRE'S BABY
Texas Cattleman's Club: Blackmail • by Andrea Laurence
Thirteen years after their breakup, Deacon Chase and Cecelia Morgan meet again...and now he's her billionaire boss! But while Deacon unravels the secrets between them, Cecelia discovers she has a little surprise in store for him, as well...

#2511 PRIDE AND PREGNANCY
by Sarah M. Anderson
Secretly wealthy FBI agent Tom Yellow Bird always puts the job first. But whisking sexy Caroline away to his luxury cabin is above and beyond. And when they end up in bed—and expecting!—it could compromise the most important case of his career...

#2512 HIS EX'S WELL-KEPT SECRET
The Ballantyne Brothers • by Joss Wood
Their weekend in Milan led to a child, but after an accident, rich jeweler Jaeger Ballantyne can't remember any of it! Now Piper Mills is back in his life, asking for his help, and once again he can't resist her...

#2513 THE MAGNATE'S MAIL-ORDER BRIDE
The McNeill Magnates • by Joanne Rock
When a Manhattan billionaire sets his sights on ballerina Sofia Koslov for a marriage of convenience to cover up an expensive family scandal, will she gain the freedom she's always craved, or will it cost her everything?

#2514 A BEAUTY FOR THE BILLIONAIRE
Accidental Heirs • by Elizabeth Bevarly
Hogan has inherited a fortune! He's gone from mechanic to billionaire overnight and can afford to win back the socialite who once broke his heart. So he hires his ex's favorite chef, Chloe, to lure her in, but soon he's falling for the wrong woman...

---

*Their weekend in Milan led to a child, but after an
accident, rich jeweler Jaeger Ballantyne can't remember
any of it! Now Piper Mills is back in his life, asking for his
help, and once again he can't resist her...*

*Read on for a sneak peek at
HIS EX'S WELL-KEPT SECRET,
the first in Joss Wood's
BALLANTYNE BILLIONAIRES series!*

She had to calm down.

She was going to see Jaeger again. Her onetime lover,
the father of her child, the man she'd spent the past eighteen
months fantasizing about. In Milan she hadn't been able to
look at him without wanting to kiss him, without wanting to
get naked with him as soon as humanly possible.

Jaeger, the same man who'd blocked her from his life.

She had to pull herself together! She was not a gauche
girl about to meet her first crush. She had sapphires to sell,
her house to save, a child to raise.

Piper turned when male voices drifted toward her, and
she immediately recognized Jaeger's deep timbre. Her skin
prickled and burned and her heart flew out of her chest.

"Miss Mills?"

His hair was slightly shorter, she noticed, his stubble a
little heavier. His eyes were still the same arresting blue, but
his shoulders seemed broader, his arms under the sleeves of
the black oxford shirt more defined. A soft leather belt was
threaded through the loops of black chinos.

The corner of his mouth tipped up, the same way it had the first time they'd met, and like before, the butterflies in her stomach crashed into one another. She couldn't, wouldn't throw herself into his arms and tell him that her mouth had missed his, that her body still craved his.

He held out his hand. "I'm Jaeger Ballantyne."

Yes, I know. We did several things to each other that, when I remember Milan, still make me blush.

What had she said in Italy? *When we meet again, we'll pretend we never saw each other naked.*

Was he really going to take her statement literally?

Jaeger shoved his hand into the pocket of his pants and rocked on his heels, his expression wary. "Okay, skipping the pleasantries. I understand you have some sapphires you'd like me to see?"

His words instantly reminded her of her mission. She'd spent one night with the Playboy of Park Avenue and he'd unknowingly given her the best gift of her life, but that wasn't why she was here. She needed him to buy the gems so she could keep her house.

Piper nodded. "Right. Yes, I have sapphires."

"I only deal in exceptional stones, Ms. Mills."

Piper reached into the side pocket of her tote bag and hauled out a knuckle-size cut sapphire. "This exceptional enough for you, Ballantyne?"

Don't miss
HIS EX'S WELL KEPT SECRET by Joss Wood,
available April 2017 wherever
Harlequin® Desire books and ebooks are sold.

And follow the rest of the Ballantynes with
REUNITED...AND PREGNANT, available June 2017,
Linc's story, available August 2017,
and Sage's story, available January 2018.

www.Harlequin.com

TEN-DAY BABY TAKEOVER
BY KAREN BOOTH,

**PART OF HARLEQUIN DESIRE'S
#1 BESTSELLING SERIES**

*Powerful men...wrapped around
their babies' little fingers.*

A BILLIONAIRE'S BABY DEAL!

One look into his infant son's trusting blue gaze
and Aiden Langford knows his wild days are over.
If only he can get Sarah Daltrey, his son's temporary
guardian, to give him daddy lessons. Certainly she'll
agree to his ten-day proposal to stay as the nanny.
He just needs to keep his mind on parenting and
off Sarah's seductive curves...

*Available April 2017 wherever
Harlequin® Desire books and ebooks are sold.*

Whatever You're Into… Passionate Reads

Looking for more passionate reads from Harlequin®?
Fear not! Harlequin® Presents, Harlequin® Desire and
Harlequin® Blaze offer you irresistible romance stories
featuring powerful heroes.

HARLEQUIN *Presents*

Do you want alpha males, decadent glamour and jet-set
lifestyles? Step into the sensational, sophisticated world of
Harlequin® Presents, where sinfully tempting heroes ignite a
fierce and wickedly irresistible passion!

HARLEQUIN *Desire*

Harlequin® Desire novels are powerful, passionate and
provocative contemporary romances set against a backdrop of
wealth, privilege and sweeping family saga. Alpha heroes with
a soft side meet strong-willed but vulnerable heroines amid a
dramatic world of divided loyalties, high-stakes conflict and
intense emotion.

HARLEQUIN *Blaze*

Harlequin® Blaze stories sizzle with strong heroines and
irresistible heroes playing the game of modern love and lust.
They're fun, sexy and always steamy.

Be sure to check out our full selection of books
within each series every month!

www.Harlequin.com

Love the Harlequin book you just read?

Your opinion matters.

Review this book on your favorite book site, review site, blog or your own social media properties and share your opinion with other readers!

Be sure to connect with us at:
Harlequin.com/Newsletters
Facebook.com/HarlequinBooks
Twitter.com/HarlequinBooks

Get 2 Free Books,
Plus 2 Free Gifts—
just for trying the Reader Service!